SURRECTION

By Douglas Hemme

ISBN 979-8-9914671-4-8

First Edition 2025

Chapter 1

Hedonist

Malcolm rhythmically tapped the eraser of his mechanical pencil on his desk. An incessant tapping that would surely have touched the nerves of any audience, if there were one, in his expansive poorly lit workspace. The tapping was a nervous tick he had since he could hold a pencil. Since he could hold anything, really. It was a reaction that tapped into the rhythm of his psyche like a biological metronome. The sound of it echoed through the mostly empty room. The beat of his lifeforce.

No, not his heartbeat. The heart was just an instrument to keep the body oxygenated and the blood flowing. The heart was nothing more than a variable rate, variable flow, multistage diaphragm positive displacement pump. What he tapped into was much deeper than that. Something in the consciousness.

When he was young, the doctors who put him on the autism spectrum called it an autistic tic, or more colloquially, *stimming*. But there was more to it than that. To Malcolm, it was his mind - his consciousness - calling out to his body, in a way that no one else notices, seeking a way out. And he was determined to set it free.

It was four o'clock in the morning and the sun would be up soon. Malcolm had pulled another all-nighter, but he was so close to a breakthrough. He could feel it. This time was different. The night before, he had surrected, if just for a moment, and he had to figure out how. The culmination of his years of research, trials and errors, was finally within reach. A breakthrough that could very well redefine the human experience. A *surrection* – separating the human consciousness from a living body – initiated, controlled, and most importantly, ended by returning to the body. *The advancement of knowledge humankind could gain from this was astronomical. Pun intended,* thought Malcolm.

For years, he had been panned by critics for practicing and promoting pseudoscience. When Malcolm first created his company, Pāra, he was inundated with media scrutiny. Well-known for his wealthy family, anything he did or associated with made the news. This time, founding his company resulted in business magazine articles dubbing him a "modern day Timothy Leary" for his work with hallucinogens. Psychologists, philosophers, theologists, biomedical engineering and pharmaceutical company CEOs all called his work and his goals laughable.

Fortunately, he did not require external investors or academic approval for his studies. When his parents died, nearly two decades before, Malcolm had inherited a sizable estate, including a trust fund that enabled his relentless pursuit of separating the consciousness from the body. He was looking for an authentic out-of-body experience; not just one that tricks the mind through hallucinations; simulated traverses through the universe – merely imaginary within the mind. He wanted to truly transcend from his bodily form, detach his consciousness – his soul – from his body to explore the cosmos, and be home in time for dinner.

His venture came at a cost though. Surely the monetary cost was easily achievable for Malcolm, but the regulatory cost required sacrifice. Shunned by academia and shunned by investors, Malcolm took the brunt of societal judgment for his cause, while the government would share in any reward. It was just as well, since his aim was to share any discovery freely with the world. He did not aim to register a patent or to gain monetarily, and a government contract was a necessary arrangement for the procurement and use of controlled substances otherwise unattainable for research. The one mutually agreed condition was for the arrangement was to be kept secret, and knowledge shared between the parties, of course. On this, he was more like Timothy Leary than people knew.

Malcolm was certainly experienced in the transcendent traditions of various cultures around the world, traveling for rituals, meditation, yoga, spirit walks, or psychedelic journeys throughout the globe. Yes, he had been there, and luckily with little to show for it. No free t-shirt. All Malcolm got was this lousy scar on his right forearm from falling into hot lava rocks after passing out in a sweat lodge. Well, that and, much like the Jimmy Buffett song, a new tattoo of questionable origin. His tattoo was a mandala, though, not a Mexican cutie. At least the anonymous artist produced clean lines.

Now in his mid-forties, Malcolm's body was the aggregate of these adventures, as much as his state of mind was the amalgamation of the experiences. Undeterred by a failure to find a probably non-existent reproducible path to surrection through existing rituals and spiritual journeys throughout the world, he set about utilizing his inheritance to discover a pathway himself. Thus was the origin of Pāra.

A biological engineer by education, Malcolm's extended family kept the expectations of him high, just as his parents would have had they still been alive. Sid and Martha Wallace came from old money and had the luxury of doing as they pleased, living where they pleased, and working or not as they pleased. Still, sloth was a vice that was looked down upon with disdain throughout the family. The family money had luckily been distributed amongst the previous generation before their untimely death, and with no siblings, their estate transferred to Malcolm uncontested. What his extended family thought of him and his ambition was inconsequential. They did not understand the mission he was on, nor the journey he was taking to get there. In their eyes, he would always be a hedonist nepobaby without goals or purpose other than to spend his family fortune on pleasure. As such, he remained estranged from them. This was hardly the truth, though. His singular focus required travel and research, for what he hoped would result in a significant contribution to humankind. The intoxicating effects of hallucinogens were merely a side effect of his work, not the end goal.

Years before, he was in his final year of undergrad at Massachusetts Institute of Technology, when the news came. Pulled from class by a school administrator, he was saved from the slightly-less convenient finding out about his parents' death via a phone notification when the helicopter they were flying in had a mechanical failure and plunged into undeveloped land in West Texas they were surveying for a potential purchase. International news was quick to report the tragedy, considering the prominent status his parents had in both the United States and Great Britain.

His father, Sid, had chosen a career in finance. An obvious choice for one with more money than he knew what to do with. It was easy to apply the concepts in business school with little concern for risk when failure was only a minor financial inconvenience. Still, he created large holding companies and consolidated vertically integrated industries into single investments. Then, he would do it all over again with their competitors, essentially hedging his initial investment. At that point, the main driver for profit was that of economic growth and the only competition was recession and regulation. Unfortunately, stifling or swallowing up any competition was a requirement for this business model. Classic monopolistic practices. But with different companies and boards in each holding company, he could pull the strings in multiple 'competitors' without fear of monopoly busting regulations.

Sid could have chosen a different route. His father, Fredrick, the heir to the family fortune, chose a more leisurely life, the largest burden being the judgment of others in the family. If not for restrictions on his finances, he might have given it all away, too. Many assumed that Sid was short for Sydney, or Sedrick, or some other classic European name. No. Fredrick named him after Siddhartha Gautama, the one known to the world as the Buddha, or "awakened one." Malcolm suspected that his grandfather had a similar drive as he – to seek enlightenment.

Chapter 2

Government Assistance

Malcolm was obviously not the stalwart businessman that was Sid, but he was savvy enough to recognize the need to limit liability in his venture. This is why he created Pāra in the first place, having no intention of turning a profit. Medicinal trials on humans were a regulatory hurdle that he would not be able to surmount on his own, especially given his purpose and intent of varying dosages and concentrations of the compounds they administered. To circumvent this, all of their experimental trials were limited to two volunteers: Colin and Malcolm. Malcolm understood and was versed in the consumption of hallucinogens, and he wasn't willing to ask someone else to do something he was unwilling to do himself.

It was no secret what Malcolm intended to achieve, and the methods he planned to implement to achieve it. From the business magazine articles, to professionals mocking him, he was a well-known target for scrutiny. Regardless, he formally sought research authorization for use of controlled substances, through the Drug Enforcement Agency (DEA), virtually the moment Pāra was incorporated.

After several months, it was becoming evident that he would not receive the approvals necessary to legally perform the research he intended. Until one brisk fall afternoon, a call came in over the intercom from the front gate.

"Hello, we are here to see Malcolm Wallace," the voice called over.

"Who, may I ask, is calling?" replied Malcolm.

"My name is Colin, and this is my colleague, Macy," he said.

"We can help you with your DEA drug authorization."

After a moment, the gate buzzed, and, bisecting, began its slow inward motion to the sides of the entrance, clearing the way for the Toyota Land Cruiser to ascend the long drive to a roundabout at the front of the main house of the property. As the vehicle approached, Malcolm watched it suspiciously through the closed-circuit security system. The occupants were not only unannounced but seemed to make a wild claim as an excuse for showing up. There weren't many that he knew that had the pull to approve the certification he sought. He had already exhausted all connections that he had in his social circle. He suspected this could be an attempted robbery.

He remained in the house as the occupants exited the vehicle and approached the front door, their faces clearly seen from the cameras as they transitioned through the frame of the driveway to front door cameras. They did not appear to be armed, though one could never tell, and their appearance and demeanor did not give any reason to be alarmed. Malcolm called on Darwin, his Great Dane, to accompany him down the long hallway from his study to the main entry foyer of the residence. It was a Sunday, so the groundskeeper and caretaker had the day off.

As soon as Malcolm opened the door, the man began talking. Clearly, he was the deal-closer of the two and he liked to hear himself talk. He introduced himself as Colin, a psychoanalyst, and his companion as Macy, a pharmacologist, employed by the Department of Homeland Security (DHS). As Ronald Reagan once famously said at a press conference in 1986, the next words out of Colin's mouth were the *nine most terrifying words in the English language:* "I'm from the government and I'm here to help."

Malcolm did not believe much of what Colin said, not even his name. But what he offered was a legal way forward towards Malcolm's experimentation goals. The deal was, Colin would stream-line authorization for use of controlled substances through the DEA and he and Macy would be involved in the experimentation and have access to the results. Macy would manage the pharmacological compounding and administration of doses, and Colin would join Malcolm as a test subject.

Chapter 3

Narcissist

A short statured man in his early thirties, Colin was unencumbered by social norms and profoundly narcissistic. The Central Intelligence Agency had recruited him from the University of Kentucky after an incident that portrayed his natural ability to con others into believing virtually anything he wanted. Unfortunately for Colin, he was expelled when someone not under the spell of his scheme caught on and alerted administrators and law enforcement. The agency had been watching Colin for a couple of years already after banking irregularities were red flagged in his accounts. He wasn't aware of that fact, or else he would have suspected that his marks were none the wiser of his scheme and that he was actually ratted out by the CIA. After being arrested, a deal too good to be true presented itself to him, and as is always the case, it was. He became a CIA asset, or agent, depending on their mood. All the fortune and none of the fame, a nightmare to an attention-addict like Colin.

Hard to keep in line, his latest assignment sent him to South America, where he was able to work out some interesting deals with local governments and cartels. As was his nature, Colin flew too close to the sun, arranging for clandestine deals within clandestine deals to line his own pockets. This didn't sit well with his handlers in the agency. He was pulled from the foreign assignment and called back to D.C.

Colin had other plans though.

Cruising northbound on the California Pacific Coast highway in a red Maserati, he just might have been able to top out the GranCabrio at 196 miles per hour if the top had been up. The policeman had originally clocked him at 89 miles per hour. He probably could have prolonged his escape from the agency had he pulled over, but his impulsive nature took over his decision making as it so often does. Instead, Santa Barbara County was now the new owner of a Maserati and $5 million in cash, which would remain unclaimed.

Continuing a lifelong theme, Colin would not face the consequences of his actions here, nor learn from them. An overnight stay in the county jail ended his brief attempt at freedom. Bail was posted and he was whisked away by a pair of agents to the Los Angeles International airport for a 5-hour flight to Washington, D.C. He was not bound, but he knew that there was no escaping from his companions.

Coach. They put him in the center seat in coach. Clearly sending him a message of displeasure for his actions, yet he remained unremorseful. His seatmates were unreceptive to his attempts at conversation, so Colin had plenty of time to concoct an elaborate tale explaining away blame for his actions and shifting it to others. This is where he excelled. It was the reason he was recruited in the first place. But he knew his elaborate web of lies would fall flat in the face of Naomi, his supervisor.

She had groomed him for the last twelve years and did not fall for his charm, regardless of the charismatic, theatrical way in which he presented it. All smoke and mirrors, and she had the vision to see through it. He hated being controlled, and he hated that the methods of manipulation which got him through life, which made him successful, were useless here. He knew the agency owned him. But he wasn't going to capitulate to it. When the next opportunity presented itself, he would find a new way out of it.

When the plane landed and taxied to the gate, it was already late evening in Washington, D.C. They were met by a third goon in a cliché three-piece suit and black SUV. Colin and his escorts climbed in the back – Colin found himself riding in the middle seat yet again - then they began their descent into the belly of the United States intelligence stronghold. They traveled along the bank of the Potomac River until they reached CIA headquarters.

Colin knew his sleeping arrangements would only be slightly more comfortable tonight. A stark contrast from the 5-star hotels he had been accustomed to ever since his departure from Venezuela nearly two months earlier. This predicament was entirely his fault, but he didn't accept that fact. He was a victim of manipulation by the national intelligence apparatus, writ large. He was being used to further the interests of his superiors, with no personal gain. He wasn't patriotic enough to engage in that level of risk without substantial reward, and they didn't even feel the need to dangle a carrot in front of him. A direct shot at his inflated ego.

He had secretly purchased a cabin in Oregon nearly a year ago, under a previously unused pseudonym. They would not have been able to trace him, and he would have been able to disappear if only he had kept a low profile until he reached his destination. If he didn't divulge the location or its existence, he expected this would remain a viable option for his next opportunity to escape. The property taxes were prepaid in an escrow account, and it was secluded enough to be undisturbed for at least another couple of years.

Colin didn't know what they were going to do with him, but he wasn't fearful for his life. They wouldn't take him in if they weren't planning to continue using him. He had burned too many bridges for most field opportunities now, though, so he was anxious to see what they had in store for him. The goons escorted him to an interrogation room, without once engaging him in conversation for the last eight hours. Assuming he was about to be debriefed, he would be relieved to garner an audience for his latest imagined sequence of events. Entering the room, he noticed a pillow and wool blanket were placed neatly on the center of the table. The agents departed the room, leaving him inside alone.

An hour passed by, and Colin anticipated the door opening and the interrogation to begin at any moment. But no one came. Another second hour passed. Then third, fourth... His resolve was beginning to wear down, just as they intended, he thought. He finally took the pillow and blanket off the table, wheeled an office chair to the corner of the room - the most dimly lit area, and prepared to go to sleep. Ten minutes after getting comfortable, one of the goons came in and gestured for him to come. Colin didn't contest. He could see in his eyes, and evidenced by the scar across his face, that this guy didn't play games.

Down the hallway they went, then up an elevator, down another hallway, through another badged door, through the reception area, and into the director's office. Naomi was in the office alone. No sign of the director. Disappointing.

Colin was too dangerous an asset to be let free of his own accord or placed abroad again. Naomi was unwilling to eliminate him, so he was to be placed on an assignment closer to home. One where surely his impact could not tarnish the agency. At least not to the level the last debacle had.

Malcolm Wallace had political influence and pulled some strings in Washington, D.C., to get the approval he needed to procure and administer controlled drugs within legality. The CIA wanted to keep tabs on this, and it seemed like the perfect spot to place an incompetently rogue agent like Colin.

Naomi briefed him on his assignment. He would coordinate drug deliveries and participate in Malcolm's experiments, then report back with any results. Colin thought that this was a joke and an unbelievable waste of his talents. Obviously, a punishment for his past transgressions. Much better than prison, or worse, though, he thought. He should have felt lucky to be alive, but instead confirmed to Colin his importance and his innate talent for dodging accountability. A pharmacologist named Macy, hand-picked by Naomi, would be working in consort with Colin in this assignment. That was the deal. There was no other option that would have had Colin retain his freedom or his life.

Chapter 4

Pharmacologist

Macy was set for a great start in a career of medicine. She had an exemplary resume; 4.0 GPA, excellent work experience in pharmacies through high school and college, she was on track for her PhD and well positioned to receive a lucrative job offer from a major pharmaceutical company. It took her friends and family by surprise when she opted instead for a job as a civil servant. Her explanation of student loan forgiveness did little to quell the displeasure of her family when her career choice seemed to be the less ambitious, albeit more patriotic, one.

She was enticed by the cutting-edge work that the Central Intelligence Agency would provide, with much less regulatory obstacles to human trial. The turnaround of theory to application would cut years from the process at a U.S. based corporation. Why commit your life to lab research, animal trials, and eventually human trials, just to release the latest pill to reduce cholesterol in the growing demographic of elderly patients dependent upon the pharmaceutical empire to sustain their bodily functions until an inevitable end due to sedentary lifestyles? The corporations would then upcharge the medicines to insurance companies for the next twenty years while they hold exclusive patents, raking in millions of dollars

over the lifecycle of the patent, funneling the money to its shareholders with only pennies on the dollar back into research for the next one.

Macy was a fitness snob, looking down upon the largest customer base of prescription drugs. A tall, slender build, she meticulously cared for what she put in her body and kept to a strict regimented diet. Her sleep schedule was nearly as strict. Typically, her day begins at 4AM for a morning run, a shower before work or school, ending her day with weight training, another shower, then in bed before 10PM. She maintained this routine since high school and fully intended to maintain it for life.

She was also no fan of U.S. pharmaceutical companies or their business models. Frankly, though, the regulatory framework was the biggest detractor for a traditional career path. She wanted to see real-time results of her work, and the grey legal area in which intelligence services operated was the most suited to her desires.

The agency was privy to lesser-known qualities of Macy's. She had sadistic tendencies and a morbid curiosity to push the edges of what could be done pharmacologically to the human brain. These traits were predicted of her by company profilers in the recruiting process, but readily inherent in her first assignment assisting interrogations at a CIA black operations site. They had taken a bold step in placing her there right out of the gate, but her performance proved her worth. And her loyalty. The agency welcomed many societally shunned personality types into its ranks to perform their work. Intelligence was a dirty job, and who better to do it than people who take pride in it?

It was her loyalty that would lead her to her latest assignment with Colin. She was to assist him and Malcolm Wallace with menial hallucinogenic/sleep compounds and study their effects on the two of them, but more importantly, her purpose was to keep Colin in line and report any deviations from the assignment directly to management. To Naomi. She was the reason he was still alive. But now she would be held personally accountable for his actions. Macy was someone she could trust to keep her informed and could handle Colin, not only physically, but also see right through his charismatic façade.

Chapter 5

Transcendence

The workspace Malcolm used with his two partners, Macy and Colin, was once a guest house on his sprawling estate in Alexandria, Virginia. Once a part of George Washington's original Mount Vernon estate, the property was one of Sid's favorites. No longer hosting guests and family like his parents had, Malcolm converted the living room of the guest house into a research lab, even going so far as to remove the traditional furniture of a living space, replacing it all with a laboratory and desks for Macy, Colin and himself. One authentic leather chaise remained in the room, adjacent to his computer desk. A heart rate monitor, electrical sensors, and an IV were set up beside the chair. Computer screens were set up to monitor brain waves of the subject. This was where Malcolm conducted his experiments. Mainly on himself, but occasionally Colin would take the opportunity to… usually just nap in the chair.

The current phase of experimentation involved one patient in a medically induced lucid dream state. A range of audible and subaudible frequencies were played as an attempted catalyst to surrection. Minimal hallucinogens were used, especially compared to the amount of sleep medication, but a wide range of audible tones are emitted during the tests. These tests usually resulted in little more than a decent nap for Malcolm. But that all changed last night.

The laboratory was set up in the kitchen of the guest home. This made the most sense, with a pre-installed gas range and ventilation hood. The trio devised pharmacological compounds combining microdoses of hallucinogens, some of questionable legality even with DEA authorization, and sleep medications, designed to prime the brain to enter a lucid dream state. The reagent. They began with orally administering drug cocktails and undergoing a wait period until they took effect. Now they used needle-free subcutaneous jet-injectors, allowing the effects of the medication to come more quickly.

The addition of an auditory stimulant was Malcolm's idea from the onset of experimentation, meant to activate the properties of the compound within the brain at just the right frequency to trigger surrection. A key to unlock the conscious. The catalyst. That was his theory, anyway. The room was surrounded by Electro-Voice tower speakers, much like a school gymnasium, and the sound of the speakers reverberated throughout the home and around the property whenever they performed a test.

Void of context and understanding, outside observers would not understand what they were doing. Administering compounded medications,

attaching probes and monitoring devices, blasting out varying audible tones throughout the property, all while an inebriated test subject lays asleep in a leather chaise. Analyze, adjust the control, then repeat.

Now it was early morning. Colin and Macy had not been around since early the week before. Malcolm routinely ran experiments without assistance, as was the case last night. He scoured the footage of synchronized video, audio, and brain activity to pinpoint the moment he experienced a fleeting surrection. In a trance-like state, R.E.M. dreaming, Malcolm had felt his consciousness and body separate and he could see his point of view rise above the chair. He could remember vividly the tone playing from the sound system. He could remember the ceiling coming closer, and his sight became clear in a 360-degree view. He could see the water from the river from outside the backdoor, while simultaneously viewing the monitors and his body below him. He remembers thinking he had finally found what he had spent a lifetime searching for, then he was suddenly thrust back into his physical form with an intensity that caused him to arch his back, a gasping inhale, and waking from his dream state. He was so shaken from the experience that he did not note the time nor preserve the data of the event at the time. Hence why he was reviewing it now, slowly to see if any parameters had changed between transcending and ascending back into his body.

Malcolm pulled up the brain scans. The lead-up was typical for REM sleep, but as the auditory frequency emitted from the sound system began to ramp upward, his brain lit up like a firework - as if all synapses were firing at once. And then... poof. Darkness. But only for a fleeting moment. Then, just as quickly – he startled awake.

Time-matching the flair in brain activity with the tonal frequency, corresponding to a moment before his body arched and he let out a moan, arms extending backward, in the video footage, Malcolm identified the specific audible tone that was the catalyst for his surrection. He already knew the recipe of the compounded test serum which made for the control in the experiment. Now he could conduct another, more targeted attempt to repeat it. This time, he would keep a steady tone at the target frequency, holding the reaction, and it would be stopped on a timer – ideally returning his consciousness to his body, like last time.

Malcolm was not about to let his associates in on his experience. At least not yet. Not until he identified the correct parameters and repeated the experience, if even then. He did not trust Colin nor did he have a reason to; Even though he came through with what he had promised, he was a

compulsive liar and dangerous. He could tell that Macy felt the same way about Colin, but she had her own agenda as well. She did not work for Colin. More than likely, Malcolm suspected she was placed with him to ensure he did not step out of line. While he could appreciate that, he could not trust her either.

Chapter 6

Confirmation

There was a fog over the Potomac River the next morning. Malcolm woke to the sound of the groundskeeper mowing the lawn. It was an expansive yard, with a checkerboard manicured lawn between the main and guest houses, large enough to fill a football field.

He always slept better on the nights after a session in the chaise, but this wasn't one of those mornings. Malcolm had been up late and planned to make it through the day until later in the evening when it wouldn't be too much of an inconvenience to take sleep medicine again. He was planning to replicate last night's experiment. This time, though, he would do so in the main house. He suspected Colin was monitoring everything in the guest house. The phone, the internet, and possibly even the keystrokes of his computer. He avoided checking any of his bank accounts or private email on the computers in the makeshift lab, not like that would prevent an intrusion into his private records if they so desired.

Over the months, the three of them, Malcolm, Colin, and Macy, had spent several nights together, developing over a hundred iterations of compounded serums, then testing them one by one. Usually, they only ran a test once or

twice weekly, in order for the body to cleanse itself from the previous before starting again. During this time, Malcolm observed Colin and Macy. He was aware that they did not work for the Department of Homeland Security as Colin had claimed. That was the first of many lies.

In fact, Colin told so many lies so often that Malcolm wasn't sure if Colin could even tell the difference between reality and whatever story he concocted, unscripted. He would lie about little things that don't even matter, then give obvious lies about larger things that were easily disproved. Perhaps he did this as a power trip or maybe he did it because he thought Malcolm was too ignorant to know any better. Malcolm, though, believed it was a compulsion that could not be helped. Either way, it made him seem like a really awful and incompetent spy.

When Sid lived at the house, he installed a hidden bookshelf door in the bedroom leading to a small secure studio room complete with furniture, entertainment, a kitchenette, and a bathroom. Hard to believe (it wasn't), but there was a time when Sid had a lot of enemies. Union busting the various companies under his control was a favorite pastime of his, and for a period during the labor unions' popularity decline, union strikes against his companies had overlapped for so long, a whole year went by with at least one person picketing daily at their front gate. He had to hire security, paid for by one of his holding companies, to provide around the clock protection at the residence.   Still not completely comfortable by that arrangement, nor willing to be intimidated by threats, Sid had a large hidden panic room installed, accessible from the main bedroom.   This is where Malcolm would attempt to replicate the surrection of the night before. He was reasonably certain that Colin would not be able to monitor his actions here.

Macy had batches of the serum, #134, in the refrigerator of the guest house. Malcolm had seen her compound the batches enough times to replicate it himself, if needed, but there was already enough on hand for a hundred doses. He took a needleless injector and one of the #134 vials from the refrigerator, along with one from batches #132, #133 and #135 to just throw off anyone monitoring his actions, then made his way back to the main house.

The computer in the panic room had a rather sophisticated firewall and VPN, and neither Colin nor Macy had ever had access to it.   As far as Malcolm could tell, they did not know of the room's existence. It wasn't relevant to them to date, they spent all their time in the guest house, and even when alone, he had not given it any attention since the two of them invited themselves into his operation. Regardless, after installing a proper audio signal generator application on the computer, Malcolm pulled the plug to the outside world. The

audio output was connected to the surround sound system set up in the room, apparently set up for comfortable entertainment while the world outside descended into chaos, probably at least partially instigated by whomever occupied this room.

A rather large, soft brown leather recliner was positioned in one corner of the living area, a suitable location for his endeavor. The room was sealed air-tight, most likely designed that way to keep from being smoked out by intruders. A large rug was the centerpiece of the room, surrounded by the recliner, with a matching leather couch, loveseat and ottoman. In a vain attempt at matching the ambiance of the rest of the home, a faux electric fireplace was centered in front of the living space, with a mantel dividing it and the TV mounted on the wall above.

The opposing wall housed a Murphy bed for those longer periods of apocalyptic terror running amok inside the rest of the home. The kitchenette was quaint, but the refrigerator was plenty large enough to store the vials that Malcolm pulled from the guest house. A small pantry housed an ample supply of emergency food supplies, targeted for two or more people, and bottled water. There was even a small corner bathroom with a walk-in shower, completing the space, making it into a potential long-term safe space where the rich could survive any retaliation from the working class for denying them pensions or higher wages. At least that was the point when it was built.

Malcolm had been mentally preparing all day for what was potentially to transpire this evening. After dinner, bidding his staff adieu, he retreated to his bedroom and waited until they left the premises. Opening the bookshelf door, he entered the panic room and shut himself in. If something went awry, it would be weeks before they found him, he thought. Oh well.

He programmed a routine into the computer. A five-minute delay, ten minutes of audio set at the activation frequency, then an end sequence. To assure himself the audio would stop, he set an auto-restart for the computer at twenty minutes after the start. Malcolm paused, ensuring he was prepared to go through with this. It was something he had done several times before. He had a lifetime of transcendental experiences, but what he experienced last time was at another level.

Having satisfied himself of his resolve, he dimmed the lights, started the computer routine, self-injected the serum into his neck, and settled into the large leather recliner of his micro-fortress. As usual, Malcolm was fast asleep within thirty seconds of administering the serum. In a dream state, his subconscious had the helm. As time marched on, there were no indications or activity that would have indicated this would be anything

rotation. He then willed himself to it. In a flash he was there. Matching its speed of 17,000 miles per hour around the Earth, Malcolm found himself floating next to the space station. He looked in a window to see astronauts performing routine tasks, one reading, and another on the radio speaking to amateur radio operators on the Earth's surface.

His attention then turned away from the planet to the unobstructed view into space. He was in awe of its vastness, but there was a sense of understanding – one that was unattainable in physical form. His perception was no longer limited to the senses of the human form. He could see the x-ray emissions if he chose. He could feel the infrared. He could hear the cosmic background radiation. None of it felt out of place. It was home.

Chapter 8

Cover-Up

While Malcolm was touring the international space station and basking in the view of the cosmos, time continued at its normal pace where his body lay in slumber. He had not placed probes on it to monitor the effects of surrecting. He figured either it would work, or it wouldn't. He would return to his body, or not. There wasn't much he could do about it anyway. This was uncharted territory for science.

As the timer reached the ten-minute point, the steady hum of the catalyst sound from the speakers abruptly ceased. In a flash, Malcolm was torn from his reality in Lower Earth Orbit and suddenly awoke in the recliner. His body arched upward, inhaling a gasp of air sounding much like the moan from before, his arms extending backward again. There was a shock to the senses, both physically and mentally. A moment ago, he had been orbiting the Earth without concern for the harsh uninhabitable environment. Now he was back inside the confines of his body in a hermetically sealed room, thousands of miles away.

Nothing he had experienced in life had prepared him for this, nor could anything adequately explain what had just occurred. Malcolm once heard a term "quantum

entanglement," a phenomenon where two particles become connected in such a way that the state of one cannot be stated independently from the state of the other, regardless of the distance between them. He wondered if a similar phenomenon was occurring between the consciousness and the body during the return process of surrection.

Clearly, they had found the right combination of chemicals, combined with the catalytic properties of the auditory tone, produced the right combination to release the bond between the consciousness and the body. But the severing of that bond seemed to be temporary, so long as the conditions existed in the brain to allow it. In the midst of the euphoria of the situation, Malcolm faced a sudden panic. What would a malignant narcissist like Colin do with the ability to surrect?

It was a terrifying thought.

It was still early evening when Malcolm emerged from the panic room. He made his way across his property to the guest house and immediately got to scrubbing all information from his session the night before last. The brain scans. The video feed. The inventory of sample vials from the refrigerator. Nothing could remain which would indicate a breakthrough had occurred.

He would continue trials with Macy and Colin for a few months, then cancel the project all

together, claiming it to be a lost cause that he would like to move on from and stop the hemorrhaging of his fortune and wasting his time. But that would only be possible if he could prevent Colin from finding out the revelation in the next trial.

They had planned to trial serum #134 in two nights' time. He had to make it seem like a legitimate test without result, just like the rest, but he had to find a way to prevent it from succeeding. Macy would be on site then. It would be difficult for him to manipulate the serum without her knowledge. And as much as Colin was a compulsive liar, Marcy was equally as talented at spotting one. It would be the sweat on his brow, a subtle subconscious body movement, or the tone in his voice that would give away the entire pretense.

It would have to be the audio routine, he thought. Just take a sliver out of the progression of tones, skip right past the catalyst, and they would be none the wiser. If he did it improperly, though, snipping a little too much would cause a noticeable jump in the audio, instead of the smooth ramping sounds they were used to. Macy, being awake monitoring, would key in on the discrepancy right away. If he snipped too little, Colin would surely key in on his consciousness becoming detached from his body. It was beginning to sound like he would have to use the serum to go under and try it out at least one or two more times before then. Once to prove the upper boundary and possibly again to

prove the lower boundary of the audible catalyst is properly removed without causing a surrection. Then he needed to ensure the audio was unrecognizably different.

Malcolm could not wait to surrect again. There was a universe to explore. Boundaries to push. He needed to know all that was possible in the astral plane – the nonphysical realm of existence – now that he found and replicated the right conditions to traverse into and out of it. But that would have to wait, or so he thought, until he shook off his government shadow. He was never thrilled to be working as a team in the first place. Not any team at all, just not this one. It could have worked if he could have built a team he could trust. Perhaps some of the friends he traveled with or studied beside. Not a couple of spooks from the "Department of Homeland Security."

Chapter 9

Investigation

Colin woke from a vivid dream. One in which he had assumed a new identity as a powerful dictator of a developed nation. His dreams had become more detailed, and he remembered them more often now that he was doing trials with Malcolm. This was an interesting side effect to the drug concoctions that Macy created. An assumed identity was a natural thought progression for someone like him, who had virtually lived his life for the last decade under assumed names and imaginary identities. Secretly, he enjoyed his current position, though he would never admit it. His talents were too great to be squandered testing pharmacological compounds. It also gave him a lot of time to himself during the recovery process between trials.

Since his forced return to the D.C. area, his quality of life had taken a drastic turn for the worse. No longer living off bribery payments from corrupt foreign government officials, facilitating the illegal drug trade in South America, Colin had to survive on a fixed income from the United States government and the good graces of Naomi. He suspected she was intentionally limiting his access to funds, coercing him to access his hidden accounts overseas. He was too smart for that, though. He also knew that Macy was specifically

assigned to watch his moves. Nothing he did was done without the expectation of being observed by someone in the agency. He was most certainly being watched.

The D.C. area has one of the highest costs of living in the country, but he would make it work. It was a matter of principle, now, to prove he could live meagerly, like a middle finger to the organization forcing him into the circumstance. In lieu of spending money on furniture, Colin slept on a futon mattress, which he placed in the main room of his studio apartment in Alexandria, Virginia. This was an ideal location for commuting both to headquarters, when summoned, and to the Wallace estate on the Potomac River.

He had not been summoned, but anticipated management would see the error of their ways soon enough. It had been nine months since his attempted escape to freedom. He'll give them another three months before he starts getting restless. Meanwhile, he viewed his current assignment as a vacation. There was no daily threat to his life, nor a concern for being outed as a United States intelligence operative. Outside the country's border, money flowed much more easily, but it came with a cost. Hazardous duty.

One aspect of his circumstance he need not skimp, though, was surveillance. He had integrated sophisticated spyware, courtesy of his employer, on

all the computers on the Wallace estate. Key strokers were installed, and a secure server was in place to mirror all files – even deleted ones – from the hard drives. The closed-circuit camera feed had been tapped and sent to a secure server he could access, as well. Colin knew that Malcolm routinely conducted trials without him and Macy, and he monitored those remotely between on-site sessions. The activity he found today was intriguing.

Malcolm had done a session alone, which was not out of the ordinary, but he returned to his workspace and continued to work for hours later that night. He had never done that before. That wasn't all. He was back a couple more times the next day. Red flags abound. Finally, some action. A mystery to solve. Perhaps there would be some semblance of intelligence gathering in this job, after all. He did not believe in Malcolm's supposition, that anyone could separate the consciousness from the body, so he did not suspect he had found what he was looking for. Regardless, curiosity got to him. Colin was used to having an answer for all of his questions. This would nag at him incessantly until he discovered the mystery.

He started by accessing the video file of the session two nights before. Skipping ahead, he witnessed Malcolm self-administer the serum, then begin the audio routine. Malcolm laid back in the chaise, and soon drifted unconscious. There was nothing abnormal yet. Colin continued listening to

the audio while switching gears, opening the after-session journal each of them kept, documenting the experience through each trial session. Malcolm did not indicate anything abnormal. Rising above the ramping audio track playing in the background, Colin heard a sudden, loud gasp. He looked over at the video, which displayed Malcolm rising up from the chaise with his back arched and arms back, as if he had just been defibrillated. Bingo, thought Colin.

He made quick work of the digital forensics, piecing together what Malcolm had documented, and just as importantly, what he tried to cover up. The serum used in this trial was #134. They were to test it out together a day from now. Macy would know if he corrupted or changed out the sample. Next, he had deleted the second half of the session video from the archive. Perhaps this would have worked, but Malcolm wasn't aware of Colin's server. Malcolm had also manipulated the audio routine. He had clipped about 10 seconds from it. Perhaps he had done this because he knew they were going to be testing the serum tomorrow, Colin thought. Clever boy. But not clever enough.

Now, Colin could confront Malcolm, but that would give it all up to Macy as well. That meant whatever Malcolm had found, the agency would know. Not doing drug trials herself, Macy's involvement was an extracurricular activity. She had other obligations at the agency, so he wasn't being monitored in real-time, save for internet browsing, calls and messages. He could properly cover his tracks, and Malcolm's, too, which no one would recognize out of context anyway. He already had access to the serum and now knew the catalyst tone, if that was in fact what Malcolm was covering up. He'd just have to see for himself.

Colin wasted no time, grabbing the keys to the Land Cruiser, and was out the door. Descending down the stairs, he turned back to lock the door to his apartment. His was not a neighborhood to leave things open. A short drive later, Colin entered the property with a code and continued around the winding drive to the parking lot adjacent to the guest house. It was early enough in the day that Malcolm was more than likely still sleeping, and his arrival would not have changed that. He did occasionally come in to the "office" on days off, though not nearly as much as before he had the surveillance put in.

The guest house was dark and vacant, as expected. The door unlocked – also expected – and a not-so-subtle contrast to his studio apartment. Colin did the same as Malcolm, grabbing four different batches of serum, obfuscation for anyone trying to track his actions, then doctored the inventory lists. He grabbed a needleless injector from the medical supplies in what would have been a kitchen pantry, then he was out the door as quickly as he arrived. Five minutes, in and out.

Returning to his apartment, Colin decided it wasn't the best place for a self-medicated experiment. He packed an overnight bag with clothes, laptop, a burner phone and a Bluetooth speaker, then headed out the door. This time, he remembered to lock it.

He walked a couple of blocks down the street, picking up free Wi-Fi on his burner phone from a local fast-food restaurant. He used a VPN and a VOIP service to call for a cab and ordered a meal using cash. A few minutes later, he directed the taxi driver to Old Town and asked to be dropped off at the Old Town Alexandria Waterfront. This entire exercise was probably unnecessary, but he didn't want to make it easy on Macy or anyone else from the agency who might want to track him. He also liked the game, and continued to put his training to practice as often as possible.

Strolling along the waterfront for a few minutes, looking out for area cameras, he would periodically find one, look up and smile, just in case someone from the agency was in fact looking to track him. Colin then began to make his way on foot up King Street away from the waterfront. He watched the King Street trolley pass him by, but he wasn't in that much of a rush. He was about to check into a hotel and put himself to sleep, probably for the night. He was skeptical that whatever happened with Malcolm would happen with him. It could have been a moment of cardiac arrest, or a stroke. Regardless, he would do his due diligence to confirm for himself there was nothing more to it.

A few blocks to the northeast, walking along brick-covered sidewalk, Colin approached a large brick building with a gold outlined black sign that read The Alexandrian in gold lettering. The Old Town Alexandria hotel was named for the city founders John and Philip Alexander and built on their family homestead. Colin walked in the lobby; a modern decor subtly inspired by the Civil war era filling the entire space. He approached the check-in desk, an ornate red leather upholstered counter, topped with marble.

"How may I help you?" said the receptionist.

"Hi Stephanie, I would like to check into a room; No reservation," said Colin, after reading her nametag.

"Of course. We do have availability. How many people will be staying tonight, how many nights?" she replied.

"Just one. Just one. King bed, please," he replied.

"Certainly."

Colin handed her a credit card and driver's license. Most hotels require credit cards for deposits, even if you pay cash for a room. You just can't get by with cash alone anymore. The receptionist,

Stephanie, handed him his cards and a keycard to his room.

"You will be staying in room 420. It is a Terrace Room, overlooking our center courtyard. The elevator is located around just the corner," she said, gesturing toward the hallway.

"Thank you very much, Mr. Williams! If you need anything, please let us know. Have a nice stay!" she continued.

"Just call me Jake," he replied with a wink.

Chapter 10

Staycation

Colin's room was tastefully adorned with colorful patterns throughout, with an accent wall covered in a wallpaper of vintage lanterns. No doubt the historic motif was an effort to stay with the Old Town theme of the hotel and the district, but it seemed a bit too forced. Regardless, the hotel room was nice - much nicer than the studio flat he had lived in for months. And the balcony was a plus, overlooking the courtyard covered in pavers with tables and chairs patterned throughout. Colin shut the curtains. He was ready to get a good night's sleep for once. His outing was equally to frustrate his handlers and get a break from his modest accommodations as it was to repeat Malcolm's trial.

He swung his backpack onto the bed, pulled out and set up his laptop and connected the Bluetooth speaker. He would run a modified audio routine through the speaker, set to extend the tone that Malcolm had cut out from 10 seconds to five minutes. Next, he loaded the serum, labeled #134, into the needleless injector. Go time, he thought, shutting off the lights.

Colin injected the serum into his neck. This was the first time he did it himself. Macy had administered the compound every time before, in controlled trials at the guest house on Malcolm's estate. This is the first off-the-books trial, for him anyway. He was a risk-taker. He had little inhibition for his own safety, and he craved the excitement. This assignment had been a drag for Colin these past few months. If Malcolm had found something, anything, he wanted in on the action. He would not be left in the dark. As the meds took hold, Colin fell into a dream state, the audio routine making its rounds through the graduated tones like every other trial, until it reached the one Colin sought to omit.

In a flash, Colin's brain fired on all cylinders. Suddenly lucid and rising from his bed, he could see the room clearly in the dark, his body lay motionless on the bed and the steady tone filling the room with sound. Awestruck at what was occurring, he sought to capture every facet of the experience into his memory. He wished he had filmed this, then realized nothing happening to him right now would be seen anyway. *The bastard actually did it*, thought Colin.

Gathering his surroundings and newfound senses, he began to develop the technique for traveling. He willed himself through the curtains, out the sliding glass door, and onto the balcony. Colin could see servers below serving cocktails to patrons in the courtyard. Out of curiosity, he made his way back into the room and to the bathroom. *I'm a vampire*, he thought to himself, amused, as he viewed the mirror and saw the shower wall on both sides of him. He then made his way out to the courtyard and began to rise.

As he ascended, he could see the skyline of Washington, D.C., to the distance toward the north. A clear intent then enveloped Colin, as he backtracked his route following King Street to the riverfront. Floating over the water of the Potomac River, he veered course upstream, following the main course of the river, over the Thomas Jefferson memorial, the tidal basin, to the National Mall. He was about as high as the Washington monument as he passed over the top. He rushed over the Ellipse at breakneck speed, slowing to a stop above the White House lawn. *I'm a human drone*, he thought, exhilarated from the experience. Descending, while continuing to propel forward, he approached the infamous facade of the White House. Continuing straight through the central large bay window of the second floor, Colin found himself surrounded by portraits and blue curtains in the geometric center of the oval-shaped Blue room of the Executive Residence.

Before he could continue any further, he awoke with a preternatural gasp, his back arched sharply upward in the bed, with his arms involuntarily thrust backward. His five minutes were up.

Chapter 11

Ghost

The day arrived when Macy and Colin were to arrive for the next trial session at the Wallace estate. Malcolm mentally prepared himself to pretend all was normal, in the presence of one of the foremost experts at detecting otherwise. It would be more difficult than passing a lie detector test, and perhaps something he would have to deal with for the continued duration of their arrangement. He still hadn't figured out a way to end it yet.

Macy woke as she normally did on the days she and Colin were scheduled to go to Malcolm's. Her schedule included her normal morning run, followed by a shower, breakfast, then a rendezvous with Colin at the parking lot of CIA headquarters. They always arrived and departed the Wallace estate together. There wasn't a moment of official work for Colin that could be done without her oversight.

From her townhouse in Bethesda, she made her way to the Chesapeake and Ohio Canal Towpath by the Little Falls Reservoir for her morning run. She followed the Potomac upstream past Snake Island, Sycamore Island, Ruppert Island, and Chatauqua Island. These morning runs were like meditation for Macy. She took these moments to clear her head of lingering distractions and prepare her mentally for the day ahead.

As she approached Cabin John Island just downhill from the Clara Barton National Historic Site, she developed a sudden and sinking feeling of dread. She decided to cut her run short today and made the return trip to her home. She continued to process her thoughts to pinpoint the culprit, but continued her routine. Arriving at headquarters, she proceeded into the highly secured area from the main security gate, then approached the northwest parking lot where she was to leave her car for the evening.

Passing by the A-12 Oxcart prominently displayed at the entrance to the complex, normally brought a sense of pride to Macy for the work that she does. The CIA developed the A-12 as a successor to the U-2 spy plane. Unfortunately, after the U-2 piloted by Francis Gary Powers was shot down over the Soviet Union in May 1960, all USSR overflights were halted and the A-12 would never be able to perform its intended mission. By the time of deployment in 1967, satellites were already collecting thousands of images, and the Air Force had developed its own version of the A-12 known as the SR-71, so it did not make sense to continue funding a redundant covert program. Regardless, it stands here as a testament to the constant innovation of spy craft and technologies developed by the CIA and its sister intelligence agencies.

Today, Macy took little notice of the massive jet pointed upward to the sky as she continued to her normal meeting spot and parked her car. She still could not shake a feeling that had evolved now to one of impending doom. As usual, she was ten minutes early to their meeting time. Colin typically arrived right on time. A slight annoyance to Macy, as punctual as she was, and with more obligations than just this babysitting job.

That annoyance grew quickly as Colin failed to arrive on time. Ten minutes later, Macy tried to call him, but the line went straight to voicemail. She then pulled her laptop from her bag, accessing location tracking software, and attempted to determine his location by his cell phone and Land Cruiser. His phone was off, but was last located at his apartment. The Land Cruiser too. Neither had moved in two days. Perhaps she had now found the culprit of her feelings.

After informing Naomi, Macy made the call to Malcolm canceling tonight's session. The call was curt and direct, intentionally giving him little chance to pry for more information.

Not thirty minutes had passed before a team of four agents had arrived at Colin's apartment complex to investigate his whereabouts. If there was no reasonable explanation, this could be it for him. There were no third chances with the agency.

Everything seemed copacetic at his apartment, except for the fact he was not there. His car keys were present, but his wallet and laptop were not, indicating he had gone somewhere on foot. No indication of foul play. No forced entry. The agents, not in the know, were surprised by the meager living conditions for one of their brethren not undercover.

Naomi assigned a team to track down Colin. These next few hours were the most crucial. This was deja vu, except the fallout this time would come down directly onto her. It did not take long for them to track his departure a couple of days earlier. He could be seen on cameras at the exterior of the complex leaving on foot and walking towards businesses down the road. They accessed traffic cameras and watched as he crossed streets and entered a fast-food restaurant. The restaurant's CCTV showed him using a phone, ordering and eating a meal, departing, then entering a taxi.

The cab company records indicated they picked up a customer at the restaurant and dropped him off at the Old Town Waterfront. Accessing the local cameras in Old Town Alexandria, they found a preponderance of evidence that he had been there, including glances and smirks at the cameras to acknowledge he knew he would be tracked. The trail, however, ended abruptly at The Alexandrian. They found the alias, Jacob Williams, he used to book room 420. It would make for a quick game of

cat and mouse if he were to use it again. Colin
would not make things that easy for them, though.
After check-in, he had become a ghost.

Chapter 12

Exploration

Malcolm hung up the phone, relieved, hoping that this would be a continuing problem, whatever was going on for his associates. They'd never canceled before. Perhaps they'd even shut down the project for him.

The news Macy was canceling tonight's session gave a comforting reprieve from the stress that had consumed him as he struggled with the dilemma of concealing his discovery from perhaps the foremost experts at prying the deepest secrets from those around them.

Having prepared for a decoy session, he shifted gears and began to prepare himself to surrect again. The acquired vial of serum #134 remained in his panic room in his main residence, so he shut off the lights and made his way back from the guest house. Malcolm could hardly wait to transcend the confines of his body once more and acquaint himself with this next level existence.

Arriving at his main residence, he locked the doors behind him as he entered the house, bedroom, and panic room. Malcolm adjusted the audio routine for twenty minutes, with a failsafe computer restart at thirty minutes, then settled into his leather recliner. He would have to work on the minimum dosage and time duration for effective surrection at a later date. For now, he was focused on exploring this newfound frontier. He placed the injector onto his neck and pulled the trigger, forcing a standard dose of serum into his bloodstream. Within seconds, he was in a deep slumber.

At the five-minute mark, like clockwork, his brain synapses fired off all at once and his consciousness was released from its organic carriage. Easier than riding a bike, Malcolm immediately transported himself beyond the upper atmosphere above his home. Before traversing further, Malcolm knew he needed a landmark, or more appropriately, a reference point, before he went too far into the unknown. He had no idea how far he could travel and still return. He didn't know how fast he could travel either. He was only skimming the surface of what seemed like an infinite opportunity for learning and experiencing everything that exists.

If he wanted to travel the cosmos, he decided he would need a fixed point in space relative to his home on Earth. His home, he thought. An odd way to refer to one's body. Geostationary satellites fit his requirements perfectly. Malcolm remembered the joint NASA and NOAA geostationary operational environment satellites (GOES) in stationary orbits looming over the Western hemisphere. Concentrating, he just had to remember the right one… GOES-U was the mission's name for the last satellite launched…

But it changed names to GOES-19 once it reached orbit, he thought excitedly to himself.

In a flash, he was there, floating next to the rectangular box with a large solar array projecting out from one side. A long tube protruded from the back side of the satellite, apparently used to measure magnetic fields in the atmosphere. He was now 36,000 kilometers from Earth. A real dilemma presented itself. Should he continue on, out into the solar system and universe with the hope of being thrust back at the end of the twenty minutes of target audio, or should he remain cautious and stay within line of sight of his physical form, presumably laying on the recliner where he had left it minutes before.

Malcolm could only assume that just a few minutes had passed. He could still sense the passing of time and it seemed to progress normally. But what about time dilation, he asked himself. He had no idea if it would be a thing for his consciousness, given he presumably has no mass, but he could not be sure. He did not know his velocity, as he seemed to apparate from one location to another, nor did he know if gravity affected him at all. The combined effect of velocity and gravitational time dilation could either slow his time due to velocity or the reduced gravitational influence could speed it up, depending on the magnitudes. Given these unknown variables, there was no way for him to know how time would progress for him as compared to his home if he were to begin traversing the universe.

As Malcolm focused his thoughts on time progression, concurrently sensing time through the motion of the celestial bodies surrounding him, a peculiar thing happened. The Earth seems to slow its rotation. The geostationary GOES satellite orbiting next to Malcolm seemed to slow its acceleration, and the light intensity of the sun seemed to go down. Everything got dim. Time seemed to be slowing down. In concentrating on time, Malcolm had changed it. He had broken free from the fourth dimension.

Focusing, Malcolm adjusted his senses and could see normally again. No longer concerned with the pressures of time, Malcolm apparated back to his home to witness what was taking place with his physical form. The clock on the wall was frozen. His body lay motionless, and the silence was palpable. This was the confirmation he needed for what he already knew to be true.

With intention, he rose from his residence, taking note of the stationary cars on the Beltway filled with commuters, still in this moment of time, oblivious to his exploits. Malcolm ascended into the atmosphere with a trajectory akin to a rocket launch into low earth orbit, angled to the atmosphere, gaining in speed and altitude until he located a line of communication satellites hovering in space and time. From this reference point, he shifted direction and nearly instantaneously returned to the GOES-19 satellite.

There was so much to learn. So much to explore. The greatest limitation to doing so had been time. Before Malcolm now lay a limitless opportunity, not bound by hunger, sleep, habitable conditions, or even human senses. His thoughts were no longer confined by the biological impulses in a physical brain. He could run multiple thought processes at once, instantaneously. However, before he departed on an epic endless journey, he brought his focus back onto time.

What if time stopped?

Everything went dark. No sound, no other sensation. Nothingness. He slowed his speed to a stop. The darkest, quietest existence, completely void of any perceivable sensation. It could make a soul go mad. But this was only a prelude to the chaotic reality he entered next.

He began to move through space, but with no reference point, it could have been any direction. He intended to travel away from earth. Faintly ahead he began to see small dots. *These must be the stars.* As he accelerated through the void, the dots ahead grew brighter and other faint ones appeared in his periphery. He began to understand what he was seeing, or not: Light waves were frozen in time. As he moved, he could see them. Standing still, he could not. The same phenomenon would occur traveling at light speed. Behind you would be dark. *Space travel in science fiction never covered that.*

Malcolm had concerns about the consequences of speeding up time, though. He feared what would happen if he crossed the threshold he had placed within the audio routine. And it was a reasonable concern. Being violently thrust back into his body as he is speeding through time just sounded like a traumatizing experience. He also suspected that he would not be able to move through time into the future for the same reason, even at a conventional speed. At least not yet.

What if time reversed?

As quickly as everything went dark, the universe lit up, with the usual intensity and splendor. But if he hadn't been disoriented before, he would be now. The universe was inverted. Left was Right. Right was Left. Bright was dark and dark was bright. As time reversed, sunlight began traveling back to it, a dark spot on one side of him was the actual location of the sun and the light traveling back to it appeared as the sun itself on the opposite side. The reflective sunlight from Earth had the same effect, projecting its image on the opposite side of him as the light returned. Malcolm was absolutely stunned, watching the world turn backwards from an inverted image on the opposite side of the real thing.

As he accelerated reverse time, the light intensity grew brighter and brighter like an astrophotographic long-term exposure. The celestial bodies – sun, moon, earth, satellites – that he could readily witness began to move not only in relation to each other, but with a collective trajectory through space, causing Malcolm to consciously move to keep the same vantage point. He could not find and rely on a reference for several reasons. Namely, the earth he could see was only a reflection of the real thing, and the satellites were traveling so fast it would be a challenge just to keep by one of them.

Malcolm no longer had a reference for time as he was experiencing it. He wished he could have a watch, like the comparison of an astronaut's watch to time on earth in time dilation examples. Regardless, it would soon be time for him to return. This was the longest he had been out of the metaphysical world, even if his body was physically slumbering in the future. By the time Malcolm decided to set his time onto its normal course, he had regressed it by about three months. Concentrating, he began to slow the reversal. As the time regression slowed, everything became dimmer. In a blip, everything went dark, then was back to normal as the Earth and sun dimly appeared, returning to their respective positions in space. As forward time progression increased, everything became brighter until the intensity exceeded what was normal. Time was moving faster in the forward direction.

The moon spun quickly around the Earth three full revolutions before slowing to the same position it had when Malcolm made the leap to the GOES-19 satellite. He had returned to his present time. He was much further away from Earth this time, however. It would be a test of distance once the audio entered its exit routine. There was no longer fear of failure, though. He could always come back to this moment, then move closer. Malcolm was becoming a master of time.

Chapter 13

Hide Out

The egress from the DC area was swift and smooth, especially given his last-minute decision to quit the charade of a loyal agent. Colin left the Alexandrian on foot, purposely avoiding the security cameras he flaunted before on the way in. Carefully avoiding revealing his face to cameras along the way, he made his way to the George Mason post office and removed his go bag from a postal box. It did not contain all he needed to disappear for good, but it was enough to avoid detection and get him out of the metro area. His cabin on the west coast was still the long-term plan. Until then, he never went without a Plan B.

Working with Macy, an extremely astute interrogator, Colin knew he would have to make an unpredictable escape plan, a challenge he enjoyed. The adrenaline from the chase was addicting, though he was more accustomed to being the predator than the prey. Regardless, the added risk kicked up the excitement ever so slightly.

Colin's go bag contained alternate identification, clothes, a facial disguise, and cash. Just the basics to get into a rental car and out of town. Using a new prepaid cell phone from his bag, he promptly downloaded a car sharing app, logged in with his new identity, and booked the closest car to his location. A few blocks down the street, Colin introduced himself as Josh Bynes to the owner of a late model sedan, tank full, ready to depart the DC area.

In two hours, Mr. Bynes was crossing the convergence of Maryland, Virginia, and into West Virginia at Harper's Ferry. Bynes parked at the national historic park, taking the time to put on his new face – a prosthetic that altered the contour of his face in order to trick facial recognition software – before walking down Potomac Street to the John Brown's Fort. The brick firehouse was not much of a fort, but it sealed its place in history when abolitionist John Brown barricaded himself in it during the Harpers Ferry raid. Colin likened his escape to the Harpers Ferry raid, as he too was seeking freedom from oppressors. As such, he thought that Harpers Ferry was a fitting location for him to hide in plain sight until he could plan his next move. Downloading another crowd share application, Colin soon found himself relaxing in a Harpers Ferry Spy House vacation rental walking distance from the armory.

Colin wasn't interested in becoming a lifelong fugitive, and this time he had a new weapon with which to fight back. Thanks to Malcolm, he could now separate his soul from his body… or anyone else from theirs, for that matter. *But how best to use this,* he wondered. In truth, isolating in the Oregon mountains would never have been a sustainable option for him. He craved attention too much. Colin could hardly stand the unrewarding menial position the agency had placed him these last few months. No one expected Malcolm to achieve his mission, but it would be him who got the last laugh from it.

He wanted power. He wanted control. This would give him the freedom he deserved. And Colin could think of no better way to do that than to go on offense against his captors.

Colin prepared the vacation home for a prolonged surrection in the morning. Tapping into the security system, he set a program to end his audio routine if someone opened a door or window. It would be too late to prepare a getaway, but at least he would have a chance to fight if awake. Colin was anxious to surrect again. He planned to travel nearly sixty miles away from his body, and remain there for hours. The risk of the unknown – would it work, would he be able to return from that distance, would the chemicals work for that long – led to a rush he had been craving for all these months trapped under the agency's thumb. Naomi's thumb.

He woke early that next morning. After eating breakfast, Colin swung his backpack onto the bed, pulled out and set up his laptop and connected the Bluetooth speaker. This time he plugged in the speaker to a charger. He didn't want the battery dying ruining his entire day. He modified the audio routine again, extending the tone that Malcolm had tried to cut out from the five minutes of last time to a whole twelve hours. Some of these agents don't have much of a life outside work, he lamented, knowing he would have to stay "out" late to get the intel he was after. Finally, he pulled out the needleless injector, loaded with serum #134, clicked the play button on his laptop, and injected the serum into his neck.

Hello darkness, my old friend.

Chapter 14

Manager

It had been a day now since Colin didn't show up for their meet-up in the Langley parking lot. Macy kept Malcolm at bay, not committing to a reschedule date nor divulging the reason for the delay. She still kept her normal routine, and did not consider herself threatened by the disappearance of her associate. There was no reason to suspect otherwise, after all he had made an attempt to escape oversight of the agency before.

Naomi had no reason to shut down the project just yet, even though Macy herself saw little benefit to the agency in testing drugs on a two-bit con artist and a wealthy hippie. Truth be told, Macy liked the lab work. It was much more enjoyable than the psychoanalytic work that she performed daily at Langley headquarters. Their participation in the project, however, in whatever capacity it would be moving forward, was halted until Colin was dealt with.

A task force had been actively pursuing leads, accessing a network of integrated cameras utilizing facial recognition software, and monitoring several countries' customs databases for any potential sighting of Colin. There was no trail to have gone cold. He had simply vanished off of their radar. Confident that he did not have the resources nor the autonomy for a comprehensive escape, given the surveillance that they had over the last several months, Naomi focused the team's efforts on monitoring travel and border crossing. He had to still be inside the United States and most likely still nearby the Washington, D.C., area.

Naomi had personally briefed the Director and Deputy Director on this operation. The outcome of this escapade, if not handled efficiently and with finesse, would inevitably break her career with the agency, regardless of her connections and rapport. It was a judgment call she made to rehabilitate Colin. She'd devoted years to developing his talent and using him, which perhaps may have clouded her judgment.

Colin was like a feral cat. Some argue to euthanize feral cats because they kill billions of birds and mammals every year and risk transmitting rabies or toxoplasmosis to caregivers. Likewise, Naomi used Colin for his pernicious talents to her own ends, but now this entire situation was her toxoplasmosis. After the debacle from his last mission, she tried the trap, neuter, and release method. In hindsight, euthanasia seemed like a compellingly better option.

A graduate of George Washington University with a degree in International Affairs, Naomi Cartwright came from a family of affluence and influence. Originally feeling destined to diplomatic service, she was exposed to the intricate network of intelligence that operated parallel to the diplomatic service at embassies all over the world. Amazed and intrigued, Naomi quickly shifted her focus on the intelligence services, and with her family's connections, landed a promising leadership position right out of college.

Fast forward nearly two decades, and Naomi is comfortably in middle management of the Central Intelligence Agency. A string of operations is under her command at any given time. Her resume, the classified one, includes many operations with varied success, resulting in mediocre performance reviews and mediocre influence in the CIA. Her career is stalled, and it seems like Colin just might be the nail in the coffin. She had given it a good run, but not ascended the ranks like her younger, naïve-self had deemed inevitable. Still, she was almost eligible for retirement, and if she could hold out for another two to three years, she could leave with dignity. No accolades, as was the nature of clandestine service, but dignity at least. Then perhaps she could transition to the higher positions of diplomatic service. At least the door would be open. All that depended upon the outcome of the Colin situation. Her career was hanging in the balance.

Early morning fog hung over the Potomac River, obscuring most of Snake Island from the balcony of Naomi's home on Crest Lane. Hers was one of a cluster of newer-build homes overlooking the river in McLean, Virginia. She had it built when she began her intelligence career near the turn of the millennia. It cost a fortune even then. More than she could make in most government jobs throughout an entire career, but that wasn't a concern for Naomi. It was a prime location minutes from Langley. Walking distance if she wanted. Which she never did. The semi-seclusion and river view was certainly a nice added touch.

Today, she hoped to resolve the Colin problem. For months, she had a team tracking him, expecting him to step past the limitations of their arrangement to test the boundaries, so his conformance to the rules placed on him was a surprise. Perhaps he had finally acquiesced to continue working for the agency, she had thought. Naomi had an informal and uncommunicated plan to bring him back into the fold after twelve months of this "probationary period." She loathed the idea of having to deal with him more permanently, which is exactly what led to the predicament she was in today.

Naomi's morning routine was interrupted today. There was no time for a workout downstairs in her home gym today. Continual requests for updates from her team were no longer giving her the false semblance of control over the situation that she craved. She got dressed into her pantsuit, descended the curved staircase at the center of her home, activated the house alarm, locked the front door, and climbed into her white Mercedes-Benz G-Class wagon for the five-minute commute to Langley headquarters. She arrived to the guard shack the way she always did. She parked where she normally parked. She entered the building the way she normally did. Everything was business as usual, except for the early hour of her arrival. That changed after her morning task force brief. After that, unbeknownst to her, her every move was being watched.

Chapter 15

Job Shadow

Colin's consciousness rose out from the Harpers Ferry Spy House and continued to elevate until he could comfortably see above the mountains to the west. Below him, the town looked like Google Maps, reminding him of the countless helicopter rides across the Venezuelan Andes on his last assignment. *This will be a great way to travel*, he thought, *DC flight restrictions not applicable*. He turned toward the southeast and willed himself forward just like he had a couple of nights before.

The sixty miles to McLean, Virginia, was a lot shorter than Colin had anticipated. As he made his approach, his path led him over the Potomac River once again. A fog hovered over the water in the winding river for much of his journey, occasionally interrupted by small islands of trees. As he approached his destination, the Capital Beltway crossed over the river. Colin maintained a comfortable distance above any obstacles, as if he could physically collide with anything anyway. He was a ghost.

Ghosts do not have pockets or watches, so Colin had to figure out the time some other way. He continued past the Langley headquarters, flying over Snake Island – a clustering of trees protruding out from the fog on the river, and descended toward the Francis Scott Key bridge. Once above the bridge, Colin then veered northward towards the Georgetown University campus, finally stopping in a clearing in front of Healy Hall. Built in 1879, Healy Hall was the flagship building of the Georgetown main campus. Rising out from the center of the building stood the clock tower, prominently displaying the time for all to see. It was only five minutes to six o'clock in the morning. It was still early enough for him to catch Macy on her morning run. He had familiarized himself with her daily routine while working with her the last few months. Now, that mental exercise would finally pay off. She would lead him straight to Naomi.

Colin caught up with Macy on her return walk to her townhouse from the running trail by the river. He shadowed her through her morning routine, trying to keep himself occupied while living through the mundane tasks of someone else's life. *Haunting is even worse for the ghosts*, Colin thought. Macy finally grabbed her coat and keys and left her townhouse. As she got in her car, a grey unassuming sedan like most others, Colin put himself in the backseat. He wondered if he would remain in the car or if the car would pass through him as she drove away. Luckily for him, he went with it.

Macy pulled into the Langley headquarters, just as she had a couple days before. This time, she gave the customary attention to the A-12 on display as she pulled into the parking lot and stopped at her normal spot. If anything, she was methodical. Colin was already restless with the monotony of her routine, and was anxious to shadow anyone else whose path might cross hers that day. However, she was his best opportunity to figure out the status of the task force after him, whether or not he could even get to Naomi. Macy entered the building, took the elevator up two floors, then proceeded to her office. A small room along the wall of an open office environment, Macy's office was not nearly as organized as one would expect. File cabinets and lockers lined two walls, the file cabinets stored currently active psychological files as well as some before her time at the agency, obviously taken from archives. The cabinets stored records, compounds and other substances that she had kept in her capacity as an agency operative and pharmacologist.

Colin shadowed Macy as she logged in to her computer, making note of her username and password. Unfortunately for him, a fingerprint biometric scanner on the keyboard was required for two factor authentication. That password would do him no good without Macy. Regardless, he watched as she checked her work emails and lastly, her calendar and… Bingo. An eleven o'clock in person task force meeting led by Naomi. *Finally*, thought Colin. Now he could shed this mind-numbing fitness freak and get to his old friend and handler. His captor. Theirs was a complicated relationship.

As eleven o'clock approached, Macy locked her computer, walked down the hallway, took the elevator up another up to the top floor, then entered a briefing room. Colin followed her, finally in the presence of Naomi, the first time he had seen her since she put him on the assignment with Macy. There were several analysts and agents in the room as Naomi called for the meeting to start. There wasn't much new information, so the meeting was going to be a short one. The lead agent briefly summarized the trail Colin left when he went to Malcolm's residence, then his trip to The Alexandrian. They had not yet been able to ascertain where he disappeared to after checking in, nor could they figure out how he was able to leave without being detected. If he had a body, Colin's head would have gotten even bigger hearing their utter dismay at finding his trail. The aliases he used for the car and vacation home rentals were still uncompromised. They still believed he was in the D.C. area, which was not completely untrue, but he felt Harpers Ferry, West Virginia, was still a comfortable distance away, as long as he kept his head down. He could probably deliver anything he needed – food, supplies, etc. - for the right cost.

When the meeting adjourned, Colin followed Naomi back to her office on the same floor. He observed her close the office door and log in to her computer, noting her username and password. As an agent, he was trained to observe and memorize anything that could be of use later. That brute memorization would be especially important in this case, since there was no physical possibility of writing anything down. The rest of Naomi's day consisted of meetings and updates from other teams she was leading. He was disappointed his case did not take up more of her time than it did. At the end of her day, Naomi pulled up her email calendar, something Colin had been not so patiently waiting for all afternoon. Naomi was scheduled to meet with the director again in two days - after hours, in his office.

After four thirty in the afternoon, Naomi finally shutdown her computer, turned out the lights, and locked the door to her office. Colin followed her out to the parking lot and into her Mercedes for the short drive back to the Cartwright residence. Naomi drove down Potomac Heritage Trail, a narrow tree-lined road that ends at Turkey Run Park, a 700-acre park managed by the National Park Service. She was not going to the park, though. Naomi turned into a small residential drive. Her gate automatically opened as she approached and she drove straight in to her driveway. Colin didn't have much time left, but he had discovered where Naomi lived. *A successful recon*, he thought.

As Naomi approached her front door, Colin watched as she entered, making note of the code as she reset the security alarm. He then ascended into the atmosphere for a comfortable vantage point, and began travelling along the Potomac River back towards West Virginia. At twelve hours into his surrection, the audio transitioned. Cruising along the Virginia – Maryland border, Colin was instantly thrust back into his body with a violent jolt, his back arched, and a massive, almost inhuman moan came out of his body as he inhaled, as if he had just remembered the involuntary functions required to keep a body alive. He was now back in Harpers Ferry.

Colin was parched. Twelve hours outside of his body and his muscles were already stiff. He slowly got up out of bed, made his way to the refrigerator and downed a sports drink. He was much more comfortable mentally, though, knowing for sure that agents weren't onto his location yet. If he was going to continue long surrections, he knew he would need to do some things differently. He accessed a known online medical supplier, and purchased potassium IV bags, adult diapers, and a couple of TENS units to keep his muscles from atrophy. If he was going to leave his body unattended, the least he could do is set it up to take care of itself.

Chapter 16

Interstellar

Malcolm had been in a daze of sorts. Ever since he had returned to physical form from his last surrection, he had attempted to come to terms with its meaning and what to do with it. He continued his daily routines, but he had a nagging obligation to find the answers to cosmic mysteries that had eluded the foremost cosmologists, physicists, and astronomers. He began studying to gain context to what he might be able to travel through space and time to witness and communicate to others.

Could he witness the origin of the universe?

Was there a big bang, and was that the beginning or the end of a previous universe?

How old is the universe?

Without a reference point, time would remain an elusive immeasurable variable.

Could he witness a star collapse to a neutron star or a black hole?

Unaffected by gravity, could he pass through an event horizon, see what's inside, then return?

Are there other habitable planets? Is there life outside of Earth? Is there intelligent life??

His time was finite in physical form. He would have to make the most of it. But once released from his body, he could spend the equivalent of years - or millennia - in the span of less than a second. Without the ability to manipulate matter or interact with others, though, any significant length of time surrecting could drive someone mad.

Perhaps he had found the key to solving the Fermi paradox – the discrepancy between the lack of conclusive evidence of advanced extraterrestrial life and the apparently high likelihood of its existence. Malcolm, so caught up in his own revelations, had not dwelled long on what had happened to his associates from the government. It never occurred to him that they may also have discovered what he had. Perhaps if it had, he might have approached things differently.

Malcolm developed a plan for his first astral journey. A flyby of the sun on his way to Sirius and a return trip back. Sirius is the brightest star in the night sky, located in the constellation Canis Major. Known as the "Dog Star," Sirius was special for another reason, too. It is actually a binary star system, consisting of a blue-white star about twenty-five times brighter than the sun - Sirius A, and a white dwarf star about fifty times smaller than the sun - Sirius B. At a little over eight and a half light years away, this would truly be a test of time and distance.

After a day of research and recovering from the last surrection, Malcolm retired to his secret room adjacent to his bedroom for his inaugural interstellar journey. Cueing the audio, he sunk into the leather recliner and injected the serum into his neck. Less than a minute elapsed and he was making his already familiar ascent, rising through the house, into the atmosphere, and continuing to rise higher and higher until the familiar blue turned to black and the stars began to shine in the middle of the day.

Malcolm, having meticulously studied geostationary satellite positions the day before, positioned himself above the Indian Ocean and began to turn back time.   The entire universe inverted once again, but this time Malcolm was prepared and anticipated it. The earth began to rotate slowly at first, then faster and faster as Malcolm maintained a geostationary position above the Indian Ocean. Eventually, a satellite appeared at the exact position he maintained. At this point, Malcolm began to slow the reversal, but did not stop it until the satellite, the GOES-1, disappeared. Immediately, Malcolm set time on its normal course.

Without a reference for time, Malcolm made his own. The GOES-1 satellite was launched in 1975 and positioned above the Indian Ocean, then repositioned above the Pacific Ocean in 1978. The Sirius binary star system completes one orbit every fifty years. Now, if he could make it there, he could accelerate time to witness one complete binary star orbit, then be home in time for dinner.

Setting his sight on Sirius A, the brightest star in the sky, Malcolm focused, just as he did the first time, he left lower earth orbit. Only this time, he intended to move himself much further. And it worked. In a flash, he apparated once again. This time to the mass center of a binary star system far from everything any human has ever known. The light from one direction was suddenly intense1. So intense it drowned out everything around him. Concentrating, he was able to attenuate the brightness so that he could see again. This was clearly Sirius A. Attenuating further, he was able to discern the fainter white dwarf star on the opposite side of him that was Sirius B.

Everything he had planned for this journey was falling into place as intended. Like clockwork. For the next step, Malcolm began to speed up time. The binary stars began to move in opposite directions around him, at first. Maintaining a steady speed of time, the stars continued to accelerate in speed around their elliptical orbits, getting closer and closer and closer to their gravitational center. Speeding around to the opposing sides, they began travelling away from each other once again on the outward trajectory of their orbits. An amazing spectacle to behold, what Malcolm witnessed was exactly what was predicted in current astrophysics models.

As the stars approached their original orbital positions, Malcolm slowed time to normal progression and prepared to return. In a wholly unfamiliar place in the universe, he hoped there was a memory log of sorts to retrace his steps back to the solar system. Concentrating with complete focus, he found himself looking down upon the Indian Ocean from a familiar vantage point. This time, there was no geostationary satellite, as expected. The GOES-3, which replaced the GOES-1, was retired in 2016.

When the clock struck ten, he was back again. Back arched, arms back, with a guttural groan as he inhaled. It was becoming easier each time. *And* he was back with plenty of time before dinner.

Chapter 17

Musical Chairs

The next day, Colin set out on a new mission. He had regained confidence now that he knew the trail had gone cold for the task force set on capturing him. He originally intended to surveille his targets for days and make a well-prepared move; but he was too impatient to sit around watching others live their mundane lives, even if their days were consumed by attempting to locate him.

Armed with new information, Colin plotted a return trip to McLean, Virginia, and a visit with Naomi. It was clear she would never let him be free. Even if he managed to arrive at his Oregon cabin, he would forever have to look over his shoulder, suspecting anyone could be working for the agency. And he wouldn't be free to travel once inevitably boredom set in. Now was the time for him to go on offense.

Colin loaded his rental car and began the return trip. Stopping at a Leesburg hardware store, he collected the supplies he needed, including two combination bike locks, then continued his journey to Turkey Run Park. By early afternoon, he was hiking through the woods along the bank of the Potomac River, on his way to Naomi's home. She would still be at work, hoping her team of agents would capture him. She was about to get a taste of her own medicine.

Knowing Naomi was loath to place security cameras on the internet, Colin was confident he could approach the house from the riverbank, enter through the back door, and disarm the security alarm undetected. After ensuring no neighbors were present, that was exactly what he did. Colin then served himself a late lunch from Naomi's kitchen, and knowing her schedule, he awaited Naomi to return home from work.

As expected, the gate opened and the white Mercedes G-Class pulled into the drive in a seamless maneuver. Naomi entered the front door to her home, closed the door, and reset her security alarm. Her next intended move was to get a bottle of Moscato from the wine refrigerator in the kitchen, however, a swift hand placed a cloth over her mouth and nose. She was unconscious before she could even process the thought to resist.

Naomi awoke strapped to a chair in her own dining room with her arms and legs bound, mouth covered. A combination bike lock was accessible and, if opened, would release her hands from bondage. Before her stood Colin with a menacing grin on his face. She could not comprehend how he had eluded her team, located and found a way into her home undetected. The situation justified both her belief in his skill as an agent and her reassessed need to eliminate him at the first hint of dissension.

"We are going to perform a little medical trial," said Colin, beginning a monologue as Naomi could not reply.

"I have here a serum that Macy derived for our little project," he said, showing Naomi the needleless injector.

"You will have an out of body experience, and if this little trial does not work, you will return to your body. If it does, then you're just going to have to find another way back to the real world."

"Oh, and don't think you can hijack *my* body," he continued. "I'll have that one locked up too."

Colin injected the serum into Naomi's neck and within seconds she was deep into REM sleep. He began the audio routine on his laptop, broadcasting it through a Bluetooth speaker into the dining room. Walking into the main bedroom, he took a seat on a chair in front of a vanity mirror, placed headphones on, then started a longer audio routine from his phone. Once all was set, he bound himself with another bike lock, injected himself, and he too fell fast asleep.

Surrecting from the bedroom, Colin saw no sign of Naomi. He was only a bit curious if two ghosts could see each other passing in whatever plane of existence he traveled. He made his way into the dining room and watched as Naomi's body lay limp, upright in the chair. As the time continued to scroll upward on his laptop, he made his move, positioning himself inside Naomi's head as the catalyst audio ceased.

Back arched, arms backward, Naomi's body let out a guttural sound as it exhaled. Colin could feel the vibration causing the sound, a higher pitch and frequency than he was accustomed. He felt physically lighter. Everything seemed off. Unnatural. Unfamiliar. Of course it would. He had transported himself into a female body. Colin's gambit paid off. A life and death game of musical chairs.

He quickly removed the bike lock, knowing the combination he had set, and unbound his newly acquired body. Making his way into the bedroom, he watched his body as the audio routine transitioned on his phone. There was no change. His body was a soulless shell. A brain-dead biological vessel. He pulled out an IV bag from his backpack and set the bag to gravity feed his body. He fully intended to return to it when the time was right. Until then, he had a new body to master and little time to do so. He - or she- had a private meeting with the director the very next day.

The rest of the evening was an exploration in women's hygiene and fashion. Colin watched videos online of how to walk in high heels, how to shave legs, what clothes go together. He talked to himself in the mirror, marveling at the form of his current body. Tomorrow, he *had* to appear as if he was Naomi. At the agency, everyone is taught to identify and report suspect behavior. If he could not pull this off and was detained, without access to the serum and the audio file, he could be stuck in this female body forever.

Chapter 18

Bring Your Boss to Work Day

Luckily for Colin, Naomi had a very organized routine built into her phone and it only used biometrics to access. After the overnight crash course in living as a woman, Colin started the morning as best he could. He put Naomi's hair up in a messy bun, his best attempt at hair styling, as he didn't have the time and it wasn't something he'd researched the night before. It had never even crossed his mind to look up hair styling. He made her coffee, but it tasted off. Sight, smells, everything was off. The cold even felt different on her thin arms as he walked out onto her balcony overlooking the river.

Dressed for work, Colin awkwardly made his way out the door in the most manageable pair of heels he could find. There was muscle tone and muscle memory in the legs, but walking still required a mental skill that he had not developed. It felt like a circus talent to walk in heels holding a cup of coffee and a purse, especially when adding any other activity like opening and closing doors. He already missed having access to pockets for storage.

Getting in the Mercedes wagon, he'd hoped at least driving would be the same. It was an unfamiliar vehicle, so he wasn't accustomed to the way it drives anyway. It was not the same. The amount of effort required to turn the steering wheel alone was a big enough difference to demand his focus, lest he end up driving headfirst into one of the trees lining the sides of the road. *Luckily, Langley headquarters is less than five minutes away, but that is where the real challenge begins,* he thought.

Entry through the gate was easy enough. It was a task he had done himself many times before. Parking was simple, too. He knew where she parked, the route she took into the building, how to traverse the corridors and elevator to get to Naomi's office. Successfully avoiding any prolonged conversations, he arrived at her office, shut the door, closed the blinds, and kicked of her heels. Now he just had to go through one work day and he'd be able to get to the director. One step at a time.

Out of naivety and a strong sense of vanity, he still believed he could eliminate his problems with the agency and eventually return to his original identity and body. He logged in to Naomi's computer, utilizing the username and password he noted the previous day and his newly acquired biometrics. There had to be a way to call off the task force after him without raising suspicion. Resigning himself to the need for a higher authority to cancel the search, he prepared for the daily task force briefing. It would be a chance to show

Naomi's face so that no one would wonder where she was. He knew they had no new information about his location, so it would be a short meeting.

Colin could hardly contain himself in the small office. He was eager to yield his newfound authority. He called up Naomi's administrative assistant over the phone.

"Yes?" asked Marlene.

"I'd like a cup of coffee," Colin said. "Four sugars, no cream."

"Uh, we have the pods in the break room," Marlene replied.

"Would you like me to make one of those?"

"Sure. Whatever's available," he replied.

In an eagerness to exert authority, he was already making mistakes.

His next order of business was the venture with Malcolm. Colin dove into the project files and read Naomi's assessment of their progress, as communicated by Macy. She was analyzing the brain data, correlated to the various serum compounds, taken by both Colin and Malcolm. Macy inferred potential future agency uses for several different combinations. There was additional data fed in from black sites where they were already using some of the compounds that

Macy had developed. There was not, however, a single mention of Colin in the project files. No comment on behavioral issues, no praise for punctuality or willing participation. Nothing. It was as if he was not an integral part of the project, outside his role as a test subject. This made him livid. He was going to shut it down… now.

Gathering his composure, he brushed out Naomi's blazer and skirt, locked the computer, and made his way down the hallway to the conference room for the daily task force meeting. The same analysts and agents lined the conference table as the day before. Colin walked in the room, concentrating on every step, then took the chair that Naomi sat in last time. He then called for the meeting to start. The lead agent briefed the same story as last time, and probably every time they had met. I'm sure most in the room could recite all the details word for word by now. No new updates. Blah blah blah. Probably still in the DC area. *If only they knew how right they were,* thought Colin. Meeting adjourned.

Colin asked Macy to stay after the meeting. The conference room filed out and Colin directed Macy to close the door. Just the two of them. The last time it was just the two of them was a return trip after a session at Malcolm's, just a couple of weeks prior.

"Shut it down," said Colin, as sternly as he could in his new feminine voice.

"Uh, what are you talking about," asked Macy, taken aback.

"The Surrection project," said Colin. "Shut it down. Gather up all materials from the Wallace estate. Bring the compounds back to the lab. It is over."

"I'll arrange for a crew to pick up the equipment tomorrow," replied Macy.

"Also, wipe the files and make sure Mr. Wallace knows the compounds you developed are proprietary. Owned by the government. And he remains bound by the NDA to keep them secret, in the interest of national security," Colin continued.

Macy was surprised by this sudden reversal. The agency had maintained a fostering and symbiotic relationship with Malcolm, without any indication he would divulge any government secrets. She began to suspect that Naomi had a secret to hide, because none of this made sense. The Surrection project brought little gain, save experimental opportunities to enhance black ops interrogation techniques, but it was a minor project for Naomi to be placing her thumb on the scale. Perhaps she was feeling the heat for Colin's second disappearance.

Chapter 19

Take Your Boss from Work Day

Colin continued to scour Naomi's files for evidence of his previous exploits. He had time to kill before Naomi's meeting with the director and it would perhaps be his last chance to see her private files. His plan had so far gone as expected, but he had already surpassed his level of preparedness and the next steps were going to have to be performed ad lib. He had a handkerchief with chloroform, the audio routine in Naomi's phone, and the needleless injector in her purse. He would soon be back in a man's body, even if it was a few years older. It would come with access to much greater authority, and more importantly, much greater access to more powerful people. He had barely eaten anything in this smaller body, yet he was not hungry. He would have been starving by now. Not to worry, he thought, he would get his appetite back after the next surrection.

As seven o'clock approached, he made his way down the hallway to the reception area of the director's office. The director's administrative assistant was gone for the day and the room was dark. Colin made his way to the main office doors, pulled one open and stepped in, as if Naomi owned the place. The director was sitting in one of two lounge chairs along the side of the office, separated by a small table which seemed to be frequented by whiskey tumblers as often as a table at the local pub. He was dressed in a formal tuxedo and putting on his dress shoes. The director looked up at Naomi.

"What in the hell is going on, Naomi," Monty said. "If you don't close the loop on this Colin situation, I'm going to be forced to call in help," he continued. "Dig deeper and find this bastard."

Colin approached the sitting area, picked up the director's Scotch and downed it. He pulled out the cloth from Naomi's purse and, before he could react, thrust it over the director's mouth and nose. Colin didn't like being admonished, especially for not having had himself captured or killed yet. He pulled out the needleless injector and injected the serum into the director's neck. The chloroform was a necessary addition. Colin wasn't sure if he could administer the serum fast enough to take affect before the director could fight back. He would have had a rough time fighting a man of his stature from Naomi's body. He possibly could have done without it, but that would have been an unnecessary risk.

Colin locked the doors to the office, and began the audio routine on Naomi's phone, placing it on the table. He selected a five-minute sequence and started it. Sitting down in the chair near the director, he injected the serum into his own neck, Naomi's neck. Soon, they were both asleep. When the catalyst tone reverberated from Naomi's phone, they both surrected.

Colin, becoming quite seasoned at this, slowly moved outward from Naomi's slouched over body. He made note of the time on the phone and decided to roam the hallways of the building to ensure limited witnesses for what comes next. He returned with a minute to spare, then positioned himself in the director's head.

Back arched, arms backward, Monty's body let out a guttural sound as he exhaled. Colin could feel the vibration causing the sound, a deeper pitch and frequency than Naomi's. He felt heavier. Everything still seemed off. Unnatural. Unfamiliar. Of course, it still would. He transported himself into an older, larger man's body. A life and death game of musical chairs.

Colin grappled with the foreign nature of his new body once again. Glad to be out of heels, though, and this body felt closer to his original than the last. He promptly got up and observed Naomi's body, still and slouched over as before. He picked her up, wrapping his arms around her chest, under her armpits from behind, and dragged her inanimate body out of the office, through the reception area, and across the hallway to a breakroom – a better spot for her to be found. In the interior pocket of the director's sport coat,

Colin found an invitation to a charity event at the Smithsonian.

Chapter 20

Imposter

When the phone rang, Malcolm had been consumed with studying the known exoplanets and likelihood of habitability and potential for life. Macy called with yet another a brief and curt message, this time, that the project was being shut down. He would have to make his own path forward, but without any of the research they had jointly developed. There was no argument from him, as if he had any standing to fight against the national intelligence establishment.

He assessed his consumption rate and supply of serum #134, and determined he would have about fifty more sessions before he would have to seek out new ingredients to compound. Now that he had broken free of the confines of time, each one of those could last a lifetime if he wanted it to. Malcolm was ambivalent about the work being shut down. He was now free to continue on his solitary path of understanding and witnessing the universe, but there was less legitimacy and formality to things now.

Not to be a total recluse, Malcolm maintained many of his social obligations. Tonight, he was to attend a fundraiser event at the Smithsonian. The director of the Central Intelligence Agency, Monty, was a family friend who Malcolm suspected had assisted in getting the DEA approvals for the Surrection project, was usually in attendance at these fundraisers as well. Perhaps he would shed some light on what was going on at the agency. Something was happening.

Malcolm donned one of his tuxedos and took advantage of the occasion to drive his Aston Martin Vanquish, a present he gave to himself when he started Pāra. The drive into the city was not difficult late in the evening. It was an unusual time for events, but the organizers wanted to target the mature wealthy socialites with the invite. They hit their mark. He pulled the Aston Martin into the circular drive at the front of the Smithsonian National Museum of American History and handed the keys to the valet driver. Inside, he attempted to mingle as much as he could stand. Eventually, while taking on a predominantly line-free role in a conversation with an older couple who maintained lifelong membership with the Smithsonian, he spotted Monty walk into the museum. Giving him time to acclimate to lay of the land inside the makeshift museum venue, Malcolm approached Monty.

"Good to see you, Monty, it's been a while," said Malcolm.

Monty shot him an uncharacteristic, menacing grin.

"Malcolm, you've been busy," Monty replied.

"Thanks to you, I suspect," said Malcolm. "But apparently that is ending. Anything you can share about that?"

"You'll find out very soon," Monty said threateningly. "Good evening," he finished the conversation sharply and moved on to another.

Malcolm was disturbed by the interaction. He had known Monty since he was a child. Monty always maintained a serious demeanor and was never confrontational with him - the exact opposite of what he had witnessed tonight. It was as if Monty was possessed, or under the influence of something. He wondered at what capacity Monty was involved in the sudden stoppage of his project. Malcolm cut the night short, just as Monty had cut their conversation. The valet brought his bright red two-seater sports car to the front of the museum and Malcolm headed back to the relative safety of the suburbs.

Chapter 21

Fallout

Early in the morning, cleaning staff discovered Naomi unresponsive in the break room. They promptly notified security, who called 911 and requested medical assistance. She was transported to the nearest hospital. The doctors could not identify anything physically wrong with her. She seemed catatonic, brain dead. They ran toxicology panels and came up with some unexplainable results, but none that indicated a cause.

An anonymous call led law enforcement to perform a wellness check at the Cartwright residence. There, through the balcony window, they could see a body slumped over in the master bathroom. They made a forced entry into the home and discovered an unresponsive male subject in the bathroom. An ambulance arrived and a medical team transported him to the nearest hospital. When it was discovered that the unidentified male subject was in the residence of the female subject showing the same symptoms, both were placed into quarantine until it could be determined that whatever caused their state was not contagious.

News of Naomi and Colin's fate quickly spread inside the agency, as would be expected in any intelligence organization. There was no ambiguity at the agency of the identity of the unidentified person at Naomi's residence, though law enforcement was not so quick to catch on. That morning, Macy requested a meeting with the director. Colin had the director's assistant clear Monty's schedule to meet with her.

"Director, thank you for meeting with me," said Macy as she walked into his office.

"Good morning, Macy, how can I help you," Colin said with a grin and an uncanny care-free tone.

Taken aback, Macy replied, "I am concerned that the situation with Naomi and Colin may have something to do with Project Surrection, which Colin and I were assigned."

"What makes you think that," asked Colin.

"Yesterday, Naomi directed me to immediately shut down the project," she said.

"This behavior was uncharacteristic of her. She normally deals with these things herself, and I suspected that she had a reason for not dealing with it directly."

"I recommend directing the established task force to investigate this," Macy concluded.

Colin stared intensely at Macy, clearly deciding how best to respond.

"Macy, it seems that you were the only agent directly tied to both of the potential victims," Colin said with a hostile tone.

"You reported Colin missing, did you not," Colin said. Without giving her a chance to answer, he continued.

"Macy, you are to be placed on administrative leave until this investigation is over."

"Leave all of your things. Especially anything from Project Surrection," he finished.

Colin requested an agent escort Macy to her office to collect personal items only, then off premises, where her access would be temporarily revoked. *That could not have gone better if I had planned it,* thought Colin smugly. His next order of business was to reassign a leader to replace Naomi and redirect the task force to other more pressing assignments. There would be no agency investigation of Naomi or Colin. As far as they were concerned, these were isolated medical incidents of a personal nature and the agency will have no part in it.

Once she was out of the building, Colin personally made his way to Macy's office. Searching through her cabinets, he located the serums that had returned from the Wallace residence. He removed two of the four remaining vials of serum #134 and placed them in his pocket.

He now had more than enough serum to surrect hundreds of times. And thanks to his anonymous call to the local police department, his body would be taken care of under quarantine at the local hospital until he had the opportunity to retrieve it.

Chapter 22

Discovery

Alpha Centauri is collectively the fourth-brightest star in the night sky. At only four light years away, it is also the closest to our own star system. Although documented as early as 150 A.D., it wasn't until the late 1600's that astronomers discovered it was made up of multiple stars. In actuality, Alpha Centauri is a triple-star system consisting of Alpha Centauri A and Alpha Centauri B – a binary star system, with a third and fainter component star, Alpha Centauri C – or Proxima Centauri, which wasn't discovered until 1915.

Astronomers have detected a total of five planets in the Alpha Centauri system. The most probable of these to be habitable is Proxima Centauri b. Discovered in 2016, Proxima Centauri b is considered a Super Earth, having a similar mass but slightly larger radius. The planet sits just five percent of the distance from its star as the Earth does, but it is still in the habitable zone because of the low-energy output of the star. Proxima Centauri is a red dwarf star with a mass only fourteen percent of our sun, but thirty-three times denser.

Malcolm decided this would be his first exoplanet journey. *Second star to the right, then straight on till morning.* One star at a time. And then a return trip and reset. Without somehow star charting from Alpha Centauri, it would be impossible for Malcolm to navigate from one exoplanet to another. It was certainly not something he could think through on the fly.

Still disturbed by Monty's cryptic threat the night before, Malcolm sat down to a hot breakfast and turned on the local news. Morning commute traffic and weather forecasts were interrupted by local commercials, with a news teaser about a curious and mysterious pair of related incidents in which two people, a female and a John Doe, are now in comas. Malcolm felt tingles on the back of his neck. *More details at eleven o'clock.*

Malcolm was kicking himself for not seeing it earlier. Colin disappeared as soon as he had finally discovered the right conditions for surrection. He took that to be a convenient coincidence, but that was very naïve. Colin was closely monitoring everything about the project, just as he was trained to do as an intelligence operative. Malcolm's poor job as covering up his discovery was especially poor considering who he was trying to hide it from.

Malcolm had been so busy looking skyward and backward, he did not see what was going on here on the ground right now. *What has Colin been doing this past week,* he wondered. Perhaps it was the agency itself that discovered it. That would explain Macy's abrupt cancellation of the project and confiscation of all the serums and computers. That could also have explained Monty's cold attitude. Whatever Colin or the agency had done, Malcolm felt like he shared in the blame, and he would have to find out what that was for himself.

For the first time in this endeavor, Malcolm became fearful. He believed both Colin and Macy were in comas. Logic would suggest that, if it was intentional, he would be the next target. Regardless, once he surrected, no one could touch him until he came back. He would figure out what was happening and return in seconds, in the safety of his panic room. And he fully intended to find out.

He wasted no time after breakfast, without consideration to even change his clothes, Malcolm went to his bedroom and entered the panic room. He set up the audio, hopped into the recliner and injected the serum into neck. Down, out, and out. Flying out of his skin, he rose above his Mount Vernon neighborhood and made a straight line for the Langley neighborhood of McLean.

Under the early morning sun, Malcolm spotted a tow truck in the CIA headquarters parking lot removing a car from a reserved spot near the building entrance. Concentrating, Malcolm reversed time in one swift motion, regressing a whole day. As he watched, the white Mercedes G-Class wagon pulled into the parking spot. A woman

– not Macy – awkwardly exited the vehicle, then cautiously began to make her way towards the building. Regressing time once more, he found himself witnessing the evening before. The same woman made methodic confident strides, with little thought of technique, from the building to the same car. Malcolm placed himself in the car as Naomi made the short drive home.

The gate opened and the white Mercedes G-Class pulled into the drive in a seamless maneuver. With Malcolm close behind, Naomi entered the front door to her home, closed the door, and reset her security alarm. Malcolm watched in horror as Colin appeared from behind her, placing a cloth over her mouth and nose, rendering her unconscious. Colin dragged her unconscious body to a dining room chair and bound her arms and legs, then covered her mouth. He used a combination bicycle lock to bind the hands. Malcolm still did not know who she was.

Colin with a menacing grin on his face.

"We are going to perform a little medical trial," said Colin.

"I have here a serum that Macy derived for our little project," he said, brandishing a needleless injector.

"You will have an out of body experience, and if this little trial does not work, you will return to your body. If it does, then you're just going to have to find another way back to the real world."

"Oh, and don't think you can hijack *my* body," he continued. "I'll have that one locked up too."

Colin injected the serum into Naomi's neck and within seconds she was deep into REM sleep. He began the audio routine on his laptop, broadcasting it through a Bluetooth speaker into the dining room. Walking into the main bedroom, he took a seat on a chair in front of a vanity mirror, placed headphones on, then started a longer audio routine from his phone. Once all was set, he bound himself with another bike lock, injected himself, and he too fell fast asleep.

Malcolm could only watch as Naomi's body lay limp, upright in the dining room chair and Colin's was slumped over the vanity in the master bathroom. As the time ran out on the audio of Colin's laptop, Naomi let out a guttural sound as she exhaled, her back arched, and arms straight backward. Without hesitation, she removed the bike lock and unbound herself. Surprisingly, she appeared to show no signs of trauma from the experience. Malcolm watched as she made her way into the bedroom, then they both watched Colin's body remain motionless as the audio routine transitioned on his phone. His body remained slumped over. Naomi pulled out an IV bag from a backpack and set the bag to gravity feed the body.

Malcolm tried to process what he had just witnessed, but he was in a metaphorical shock. Colin had surrected, forced another person into surrection, then hijacked her body. This was perhaps the most egregious use of *his* discovery Malcolm could think of. Tearing someone from their body, into surrection, without any understanding or context, then forcibly taking over their body, leaving them in a nonphysical plane of existence for perhaps eternity. A horrendous act to inflict upon another being – one worse than murder. And given the fact that two people were reportedly in *comas*, he had likely done it again.

If he had a gut, it would have had a sinking feeling. The only thing he could do at this point is see it to the end. Malcolm jumped forward in time, watching as Colin learned to operate his new feminine form. He watched as Colin woke and followed him to Langley headquarters. Huddled in Naomi's office for most of the day, he watched as Colin fumbled his way down the hallway, participated in the task force meeting to find himself, and directed Macy to shut down their project. Then he watched as Colin assaulted Monty, forced them both into surrection and stole his body, just before the charity event at the Smithsonian. It all came full circle.

All this time, as Malcolm had been consumed with witnessing the mysteries of the universe, Colin had been planning atrocities against others including a close family friend. He had to see how far this went. To do that, Malcolm would have to do what he had been careful to avoid thus far. He would have to jump his timeline and travel to the future. Where does this rabbit hole lead? Focusing with deliberate intent, Malcolm apparated.

Chapter 23

Per Tempus

The director's office at Langley headquarters was unoccupied. By all accounts, it looked the same as it had a moment before, from Malcolm's perspective, save for new furniture and décor. Curiously, the computer monitor was gone. New portraits hung along the back wall displaying past directors, with the current director and the President of the United States, prominently displayed in the center. The images seemed to sink into the frames, presenting three dimensional images staring back into the room. Their names, C3asera Dizer0 and Hym3n G8Men, respectively, included an odd combination of characters including numbers and uppercase letters, as if they had run out of combinations for usernames. Their clothes looked more like jumpsuits than the traditional three piece or business suit. He couldn't be sure which comparison applied, as their appearance looked quite androgynous. There appeared some utilitarian aspect to the clothing, though.

The former of the two, labeled C3asera on their portrait, burst into the room, disrupting Malcolm's solemn reflection of his surroundings. They were dressed similarly to the portrait, hair combed to one side, with a mask hanging toward the other. *There must be pollution or atmospheric problems*, thought Malcolm, as he observed the functionality of the fashion. C3asera continued talking to another person as they both entered the room.

"The Middle East situation isn't a new one," C3asera said.

"This conflict has been going on for centuries," C3asera continued.

"Our friends are quite concerned for the safety of their families," said the companion.

"Look Senator, if you want a quick solution to the current uprising, contact Pāra directly, if you have the funding. The CIA is too transparent these days due to your own legislation to do what needs to be done to arrive at a quick solution to your problem."

C3asera walked the Senator to the door, ushering them out.

Pāra, thought Malcolm. *Surely they were not referring to the same Pāra that he founded. And what future is this,* he thought. He had to find out what year this was. In an effort to jump the timeline, he must have overshot by years, if not decades. His first goal would have to be determining when he was, then he would have to figure out why the director of the CIA referred a Senator to go "directly" to Pāra, for a fee. That implied that Pāra was utilized indirectly by the

CIA, in some capacity to influence a current conflict in the Middle East. This was very perplexing to Malcolm. And disturbing.

Malcolm made his leave of the director's office and ascended above a much older looking Langley Headquarters. The Washington D.C. skyline seemed vaguely familiar from past travels, yet completely different. Newer, taller buildings packed the outskirts of the historic downtown area, shaped in a way that made their structural integrity seem like they defied gravity. Engineering must have had many advances over the last, however many years. Perhaps he would be able to find out what year it was if he could figure out how to access news media, if it was still even a thing.

He focused on the nearest high-rise, a gaudy structure located on the Maryland side of the Potomac River intruding upon any possible view of D.C. from the Virginia side. Approaching, he noted the cylindrical building was lined with balconies. From one balcony, he could see a holographic figure -hardly discernible from a real person - lit up in the center of what he assumed was a living room. Going in for a closer look, Malcolm entered through the balcony doorway to see a couple sitting on some new fad version of zero gravity chairs. He joined them, listening as yet another androgynous figure projected into the room discussed local news and events. There was a small ticker on the bottom circling around the person that appeared to display a date. He moved in closer to read *November 4th... 2225*.

Two hundred years.

Chapter 24

Pāra Corporation

Malcolm exited the residence the same way he had entered, out the balcony, then ascended through the traffic of personal commuter aircraft to an altitude reserved by practicality to longer distance flights. From this vantage point, he could see beyond the metropolitan areas of what he had known as Washington, D.C., and Baltimore. There was no longer any delineation between the two. It was one congruent metropolis, surrounded by a ring of suburbs. Unexpectedly, though, another region showed definition between the suburbs what few rural areas were left in this overpopulated region.

Investigating this anomaly, Malcolm descended westward upon the greyish region, making out grids of small roofs made of scrap metal, giving the appearance of a twentieth century third-world country. *These are slums,* he thought, exasperated by the realization. Men, women and children lined the dirt alleys and roads between rows of primitive shelters with no services. Plumbing, sewage, electricity all nonexistent – except for the security lights from the walls placed on the border between this and the suburban areas. The walls were occupied by security personnel wearing advanced camouflage uniforms with a Pāra logo emblazoned upon the left shoulder. All the security personnel on the wall and at the gate entrance to the metropolis were wearing respirators, and appeared to be in good health and physical shape. Very few people outside the perimeter had respirators or masks, and the ones that did not seemed to be physically ill.

"The comfort of the rich depends upon an abundant supply of the poor" - Voltaire

Malcolm surmised that overpopulation and an even wider gap between socioeconomic classes contributed to the emergence of these areas surrounding the cities. He followed the border wall, observing hundreds of security personnel in similar uniforms. Seeking to gain further perspective, he returned to the sky and descended again toward the Hampton Roads area of Virginia. To his dismay, the same slums, similar walls, and same Pāra security were there to keep them out.

Half of what was once Virginia Beach was now Atlantic Ocean, and the Outer Banks in North Carolina no longer existed. The Chesapeake Bay Bridge Tunnel, which once consisted of a group of tunnels and bridges spanning the entrance to the Chesapeake Bay, had been replaced by an elaborate system of levees and locks in a monumental effort of engineering to keep the rising sea levels at bay. It appeared to be working thus far – keeping out the poor from one side, and ocean water from the other.

Pāra appeared now to be, among other things, a hired protection force to keep the impoverished from entering the cities. Extrapolating this out to the major cities in the United States alone, Pāra must employ an army of hundreds of thousands of mercenaries, if that was the limitation of its reach.

Rising above the airline jet routes, Malcolm made his way out of the atmosphere and into low earth orbit, continuing his trajectory through an area crowded with satellites whose orbits seem to be meticulously planned and executed, lest they cause a cascade of collisions. Low earth orbit was so crowded with satellites traveling in single file rows in each orbit – many sporting the Pāra logo – providing continual services on the Earth' surface, that he could not imagine how any new space flights took place without collisions. Once he reached the altitude equivalent to geosynchronous orbits, Malcolm stopped beside a geostationary satellite where the GOES-19 used to orbit. The GOES, he assumed, had been pushed into an outer orbit after its useful life was over, probably over a hundred and fifty years earlier.

He took this opportunity to reflect on a twenty-third century Earth below him. The oceans had swallowed up much of the coastal regions throughout the globe. Areas where he once saw green were now the brown hues of deserts. A few areas had gone the opposite direction – deserts to green – though not nearly enough to counter. Metropolitan areas had grown so large that they could be seen as dark spots on what was left of the land mass, blemishes on the face of the Earth. Pollution could be seen emanating from these dark spots. It seemed that people with the power had yet to make the inconvenient choices required to mitigate harm to our planet, so long as it was only those without the control who suffered the consequences. It appeared as if we had learned nothing in the last two hundred years.

Chapter 25

Pāra Military

From New York City to Los Angeles, Houston, Philadelphia, Chicago, Phoenix, the same situation played out. Pāra soldiers lined the walls of the great metropolitan areas, controlling passage into and out of the cities. Likewise, a similar wall spanning hundreds of miles now lined the southern U.S. border. Armored vehicles with the Pāra logo patrolled this vast expanse as well.

U.S. military bases now flew a Pāra flag just below the American one, and were filled, not with Army, Marines, Navy, Coast Guard, Air Force, or Space Force personnel, but with Pāra mercenaries. The United States military had been privatized.

As Pāra built out its private militarization portfolio, signing long term contracts with the United States, and subsequently all the countries in NATO, the North Atlantic Treaty Organization, the threat of war between countries became less and less, until the final country signed a protection contract with Pāra.

Pāra would never attack itself in the interest of any nation, contract or not. But it *would* take for itself the defense budgets of all nations. To justify the largest military force the world has ever seen,

Pāra had to continue to foster fear of foreign nonstate actors and to maintain class warfare, oppressing the poorest by scaring the wealthy and elite into believing that their enormous wealth might be taken by force.

Pāra sailors patrolled the coastal waters, and Pāra astronauts guided spacecraft through the crowded lower earth orbit for commercial, government, and private space flights. Pāra pilots patrolled the skies and protected the restricted airspace surrounding all the major metropolitan areas. Pāra spies embedded in political and activist groups, while Pāra mercenaries hunted criminals and terrorist groups. There were no restricted boundaries in which they operated and extradition was a thing of the past.

The United States was not exclusive or even an outlier in its descent into this dystopian landscape. In Mexico City, Toronto, Ottawa, Paris, Tokyo, Moscow, New Delhi, Shanghai, Berlin, London, Istanbul, Jakarta, São Paulo, and every other major city across the globe, Pāra soldiers roamed the streets. This was the new world order.

Countries were beholden to Pāra for maintaining the dichotomy between the wealthy and the impoverished. This was now a driving revenue generator for Pāra corporation – cultivating class warfare

As "luck" would have it, intelligence services became privatized as well, with no-bid contracts landing into the hands of Pāra executives. The CIA was relegated to nothing more than an administrative organization Significant lobbying led to this transition of world power, but there were benefits, such as ending violent conflicts between nations and eliminating the potential for nuclear war.   With little threat of external enemies, intelligence turned inward, policing and controlling the domestic populations.

No more wars. Unlimited power.

Chapter 26

Mount Vernon

Malcolm imagined all the things that had taken place to change the world that he knew to the one he was witnessing now, and the geopolitics that had to have taken place to land *his* company as a dominant world influencer. It was not a direction he would have taken with his lifelong pursuit. Something horrible must have happened, perhaps after he died, or perhaps someone had taken the name, or perhaps that bad thing was the cause of his death, he thought as he shuddered. Afterall, the repercussion of surrection was the concern that led him to the future in the first place. And there was only one prime suspect who knew his company and knew of surrection, that led him here: Colin.

Finding out the history of Pāra, Malcolm knew, would likely answer the question he traveled two centuries to find out: *What happened to Colin.* Obtaining information only by witnessing, without a physical form to manipulate anything, was a daunting task, or at least one that requires creativity. Malcolm needed to know the real history of Pāra, but he didn't even know where to find it at this point in the timeline. His best bet, he figured, was to return to the origin: his residence at Mount Vernon, Virginia, on the banks of the Potomac River.

Returning to the Potomac below, Malcolm weaved his way from the D.C. border downstream toward his old home. The trees lining the water had long been removed to make way for development. The riverwalk, which used to consist of forested jogging trails was now full of shops and pavement, harkening back to a nineteenth century Seine River in Paris, France. Making his way down river past a newer, presumably more efficient, hydroelectric plant and newer interstate bridges that did not exist in his time, Malcolm arrived at his family's estate.

Many of the houses surrounding the property had been demolished or upgraded and a large privacy fence had been erected around the property and surrounding lots. It had been turned into a secure compound. An elaborate security gate with guns trained on the entrance was placed where his unassuming entrance gate once stood. Oddly, the main residence and guest house stood just as they had the last time he had seen them - as it stood now in his own timeline with his body motionless, yet alive, waiting on his return. There was a new building on the property in one of the adjacent lots that used to house his neighbors. This building resembled a warehouse, with office space, and was adorned with large illuminated red letters spelling out Pāra. *What have I done,* Malcolm thought, as he gazed upon this enigma?

The security of the facility, though completely unmanned, seemed to be quite heavy, with both automated detection and repulsion. There were balloons in the air on the perimeter, with platforms on the top of them, holding menacing drones that appeared to have integrated weapons systems protruding from their fuselage. Machines along the perimeter appeared to be filtering the air of the surrounding area, a luxury not afforded to most in the area. There was what appeared to be personal vehicles at the front of the warehouse and the main residence, but the guest house seemed empty. Malcolm descended upon his now historic guest home.

The entry was the same as Malcolm remembered, down to the light blue color of the porch. The only noticeable difference was the door lock which was upgraded to an electronic device with a tiny red light akin to badge readers at hotels in the early twenty-first century. As he passed through the doorway, Malcolm entered a living space straight from his own time. The furniture was pristine, and frames displaying pictures of various people in locales around the world were displayed prominently on the walls as well as the mantle of the fireplace. It seemed quite out of place as compared to the apartment he had just departed. In fact, it was quite museum-like.

The pictures were a curiosity. Surely society had moved on from printed photos in the last two centuries, yet the wall was adorned with a motley crew of characters, which obviously weren't of biological lineage. Groups of all ethnicities seemed to be included in the collage: Asians, black, Caucasian, Hispanic, Middle Easterners. Malcolm's attention then moved to the mantle and he froze with shock. His own portrait was the centerpiece above, but the frames below displayed photos of Monty, Naomi, and… Colin.

Suddenly hyper-aware of his surroundings, Malcolm felt an irrational danger, irrational given that he could not be harmed in his non-physical form. Regardless, he scanned the room frantically for any clues as to what was happening - or had happened over the last two hundred years. He could not get the answers he was looking for here. Malcolm decided he would go to the main residence.

As he crossed the grounds, the estate seemed as familiar to him as it always had been. The grounds were manicured and kept immaculate still, with grass and landscaping and plants that seemed bioengineered to thrive in this more polluted environment of the twenty-third century. Interrupting his nostalgia, he pondered the possibility of his life going a different direction. It could have been him developing the flora and fauna for the elite to enjoy in this world of pavement and skyrises. But he could have also developed much-needed plants to filter out the harmful wastes placed into the air from these activities, which could have led to a more habitable world which did not require additional breathing assistance. By this point, lost in his thoughts, Malcolm arrived at the driveway in front of the main residence.

The main residence, like the guest home, remained unchanged from the decor and furnishings from his time - another odd clue to Malcolm. The kitchen was updated to modern appliances, making it obvious the house continued to be used as a residence for someone. His bedroom remained much the same, with updated mattress and bedding, but his furniture remained. Malcolm began to wonder why someone would go to such an effort to maintain a residence as if they were living two hundred years in the past - especially one with the resources that this one did. Malcolm passed through the bedroom to the adjacent panic room - his personal base of operations, and where his body lay two hundred years into the past.

This room, hidden from the relics of the past covering the rooms in the rest of the house, was modernized. Three dimensional landscapes lined the walls, and there was no longer any screen in the room at all. Seating areas were all updated to what he assumed were the latest available. The centerpiece of the room was a zero-gravity chair much like the ones he saw in the apartment he invaded to find out how far he had leapt into the future. In that chair was a young Asian man in his twenties, laid back with his eyes closed. The room was filled with ambient sounds, presumably designed to help him sleep. Notably missing from the room was his own physical form.

The shirtless man appeared to be sleeping. His hair came down to his shoulder, an undercut shaved close to the skin, with his hair pulled over just to the left side, like C3asera's. This appeared to likely be the popular utilitarian hairstyle of the era. From the waist down, he appeared to be wearing a traditional Scottish kilt, which looked out of place when judged by twenty-first century standards.

Rather than wait for his unwitting host to wake, Malcolm decided more clarity would be gained by venturing into the Pāra warehouse where his neighbors home once stood. He ascended the residence just as he had each time before, rising into the second story above his bedroom, then out the roof of the structure until he had an aerial view of the compound. He then ascended toward a cluster of windows on the corner of the Pāra building, presuming them to be offices.

His presumption was soon found to be correct as he entered an elaborate corner office on the fourth and top floor of the building. A large leather chair sat before him as he crossed through the window, facing a large ornate desk made of dark wood, presumably mahogany. Malcolm guessed that the tree that made it was still standing in some South American forest during his own lifetime. A mahogany plaque sat on top of the desk facing the double doors of the entry. Bold block letters displayed across the front of the plaque read the name Colin Wallace.

In what seemed to be a uniform celebration of the past, like the CIA director's office, this office also featured former company leaders' portraits on the wall. There were dozens of three-dimensional portraits along the wall, along with more traditional older photos - almost a hundred in total. Malcolm recognized most of them from the pictures hanging in the guest house. His own photo mixed in with the group, the diversity was again surprising, but not just the ethnicity or gender. The age ranges varied widely, but most of the recent ones seemed to be younger - in their early twenties - and more physically fit than their predecessors.

It was remarkable that such a company would choose such a widely diverse succession of leadership. This anti-nepotistic approach was something that seemed out of place in a company that used oppression as a business model and monopolistic practices to gain world-wide power. Regardless, it was celebrated with multiple magazine covers and diversity awards that lined the opposite wall.

Malcolm made his way into the facility through the ornate wooden double doors and emerged into a reception area, with a large Pāra logo behind a desk clearly set up for a gatekeeper. The waiting area consisted of large leather chairs that appeared to be too plush to have ever been sat in. It did not appear like there was much traffic into the office, ever, but especially this evening given there was no one present, inside or out. *Most business these days surely takes place remotely,* thought Malcolm. He couldn't help but think back to the "vintage" furniture of the residences as he made his way through the reception area.

Along the hallway, a half dozen other offices lined the walls. He made his way beyond them to an elevator, ascended the shaft for what he estimated to be eight floors down, and exited through what would have been the service door had the elevator been down there. He emerged into yet another unoccupied space - a hallway with four laboratory rooms with glass lined walls. There were noticeably no windows on the floor. Each room housed all the makings of a doctor's examination room - a stainless steel reclining chair, a sink and cabinet above it with medical supplies, and a refrigerator with glass doors displaying various vials of some type of injectables.

At the end of the hallway was a vault-like door resembling one inside a twentieth century Cold War nuclear missile silo, only with a technologically superior locking mechanism. *Perhaps this is where they surrect now,* Malcolm thought, seeing the secure space as an ideal location much like the panic room he used for the first intentional surrections he performed. He eagerly and easily passed through the three-foot-thick door and emerged out the other side. What was waiting for him on the other side, however, filled Malcolm with horror and disgust.

A four-story tall open space lay before him, nearly three hundred feet long. Below the entry ran a metal grated floor which spanned the length of the room, but the horror and disgust came from what lined the walls from floor to ceiling: cryogenic chambers filled with people. Not just any people, though. As he made his way along the walkway, he began to realize these were the people whose portraits hung on the walls of the guest house. Many contained the former leaders of Pāra. Each and every one of them, as he continued to the back wall. Finally arriving at the end of the row, Malcolm gazed down upon himself.

As he did, a sudden realization came over him. While he was determined to use surrection to explore the universe and seek answers to life's most pressing questions, Colin used surrection to seek wealth, power, and immortality. He systematically stole the lives of people out of greed, envy, or want of power or position, without regard for the consequences to anyone else. The room where he stood was a trophy room for all the lives cast out of their bodies without warning or explanation, for what Malcolm could only assume was a sentence of eternal purgatory. Two centuries of evidence of crimes against humanity, himself one of Colin's victims, lay dormant and frozen before him.

Chapter 27

Reminiscence

Colin awoke from a slumber in the secure room adjacent to the bedroom of his house at Mount Vernon. It was but one of many compounds his company, Pāra, maintained for his use. This one was his favorite, though, holding what could be described as a sentimental value, given it was where everything had started for him. He had been at it a long time now, as he reflected on the years he spent building his empire.

He had just arrived from his Tokyo residence where he surrected into his latest form: a young man from a dojo in the Fukushima Prefecture who had been physically groomed for the position. Pāra had funded the man's training, as they had done similarly many times in the past, with the promise of a lucrative position in the company. They always had them sign nondisclosure agreements, which required a complete separation of contact from their friends and family prior to Colin's assumption of their bodies. Long gone were the times of forcibly stealing people's identities. There was an art to the deception of body assumption nowadays.

As usual, there was a pressing matter which required his attention, and he was compelled to travel back to the United States to address the issue.

This time, it was yet another conflict in the Middle East, and there was a Senator waiting to beg him to use the power at Pāra's disposal to render an acceptable solution. Unfortunately, he had little time to acclimate to his new body before he traveled. This led to some serious jet lag and he spent the day sleeping it off. Even with a body in its most peak condition, in his nearly two and a half centuries, Colin found that the mind still required significant time to heal.

Before Colin requested the Senator's presence in his office, his signature power move - especially effective in a society where business was almost exclusively attended to remotely, nostalgia came over him. It had been years since he had last returned to Virginia. Usually, his catatonic former shells were sent back to Mount Vernon to be iced without his presence.

Colin made his way to the guest house. Decades ago, he had instructed it be maintained in the same state as it had been as he built up the company through "acquisitions" and favorable legislation in the mid twenty-first century. It was a personal museum of sorts.

Colin walked out of the main residence and meandered through the well-manicured grounds of the estate. He made his way up the steps of the porch and into the guest home using the implanted chip in the wrist of his new host, pleased that his IT department didn't screw up the transition this time. He approached the mantle with a smirk on his new face as he gazed upon pictures of his original form, Naomi, and Monty, marveling at how far he had come since the first days of surrection.

Sure, there were some mistakes at the beginning. Naomi was merely meant to be a stepping stone. Surrecting into her was proof of concept, but it was also a way to avoid capture, steer her investigation, and gain access to a higher authority. Still, he hadn't realized at the time the vast financial resources she had inherited until it was too late. He had moved on to Monty and others long before he realized that she was the wealthiest he had ever been. In truth, it was really her fault for hiding her wealth so well. She lived more like a millionaire than a billionaire. It took several more surrections and lobbying Congress for changes to living inheritance laws before he became that wealthy again. In this respect, Colin considered himself a self-made billionaire, as well as the youngest trillionaire and first multi-trillionaire.

To Colin, these accomplishments overshadowed his brief stint as the President of the United States. His singular goal after discovering surrection - an achievement he attributed to himself - was to infiltrate and assume the office of President. The ease at which he was able to surrect his way up the government structure, landing a private audience with the president, even surprised

Colin himself. It was only a matter of weeks before he was physically standing in the blue room he once briefly gazed upon while surrecting. He quickly grew bored of the monotony. From the mundane intelligence briefings, which he loathed reading, to the ceremonies, the photo opportunities signing bills that he did not care to read nor about content, it was only an illusion of the power he sought. It was the influencers behind the cameras and the media articles, the donors and the employers of the lobbyists, that held the real power to govern. And that real power is what he craved. Not that geriatric prison or stepping into and attempting to participate in a decades long marriage to an elderly woman he'd only just met.

Since he had already transferred ownership of Pāra and all his assets to the frail "leader of the free world," he reluctantly had to surrect into the man's only son and namesake in order to maintain continuity. This ultimately led to the first successful invocation of the 25th Amendment, leading to the Vice President to assume the office. That was fine with Colin. He had grown eternally bored with the job, tired of feigning interest and empathy for constituents and donors, and was eager to move on toward a revised goal of world economic dominance. The learning experience of wielding political influence proved just as, if not more, helpful to his next goal as the intelligence briefings and the additional wealth.

Pāra itself had its own accolades under his tenure. From its humble beginnings, it grew to be the largest privately held company, and eventually became the largest conglomerate corporation in the world. Pāra was now a household name with annual revenues rivaling most developed nations' GDP. Annual profits alone were above the tax revenues of any nation. With this consolidation of wealth came an unrivaled level of power and influence, even more so than the superpower nation of Chindia towards the end of the twenty-second century.

Returning from his thoughts, his pride swollen from self-listing his core achievements, Colin made his way to the Pāra facility. A cargo vehicle had arrived and it was time to inter his last body into its cryopod. This time, he would show his respects to his previous self, and put on a show for the Pāra employees, for which the truth of his succession was obscured. Frankly, they likely would not believe the truth if he had told them. He stood silently and watched as they wheeled the gurney into the vault and placed his old catatonic body into an empty pod. Technicians worked diligently to coordinate the sequence for suspending animation in the body.

The debacle with Monty, perhaps the most egregious mistake of the early days, gave way to the cryogenic storage of old hosts. A little overzealous back then, in an effort to acquire a rocket company with significant government defense and space contracts, Colin lured a billionaire entrepreneur, Nole Fetor, into one of his traps. After signing all of his assets over to his intended new host, he began the process of surrection, injecting his target and himself with serum #134 and filling the room with the catalyst audio track.

This is when chaos ensued.

At the time, Colin operated out of an empty warehouse he acquired through one of his first surrections, apparently a business venture that was yet to get off the ground before he intervened. Depending on the ruse, he would either lure his mark into the warehouse with a business proposal or subdue them first, then bring them in through the loading dock. Over the years, his process became more formalized and professional, but at this moment he was essentially a body assumption startup.

Through manipulation, schemes, and outright kidnapping, he had assumed the physical forms of all of his previous hosts and placed them in his work space, fully equipped with hospital beds and monitoring equipment. By this point, he had accumulated enough wealth to employ a simple staff of security and medical personnel to ensure their well-being. The surrections he did behind closed doors, however, without an audience.

In this particular instance, the surrection began as expected. On the re-entry, however, Nole somehow managed to enter Monty's body. Not enough time had passed for Monty's muscles to have atrophied, so this could have been a significant challenge. However, forced out of one body and into another, Nole was entered into a brief state of emergence delirium in Monty's body.

Colin had successfully transitioned to his new host's body, and he was now of significantly smaller stature than that of the former CIA director. Luckily, he was seasoned enough at surrecting to recover quickly, and identified the threat as Nole began to remove Monty's monitoring sensors and sit up in the bed. Not as agile as he was in his original form, he struggled to move Monty's larger frame. Without fully understanding what had just happened to him, Nole was smart enough to recognize the threat Colin posed and he lashed out at him, at his own body, as he gained his bearings.

If Nole had better physical control, Colin would have had a serious problem on his hands. Monty lunged at him, tackling him, and attempted to place his hands around Colin's neck. Also fortunate for Colin, Nole was a man of leisure from a wealthy family, not a trained agent. He was an adrenaline junkie, though, and the familiar flow of adrenaline ran through Nole's body and gave Colin a competitive edge. He wrested free from Monty's grip, knocking over a stainless-steel medical table and a needleless injector with serum #134 slid across the floor. Colin army crawled as quickly as he could, barely reaching the injector with the tips of his fingers before he could no longer progress any further. Monty was on top of his back again and his hands were gripped firmly around his neck. Before he passed out, Colin was able to reach behind him and inject a dose into Monty's forearm. The effects were not instant, however, and the adrenaline was not enough to fend off unconsciousness.

When Colin awoke, Monty lay next to him in a slumber. He had respect for Nole, given the fight that he gave to survive. Regardless, Colin placed him in a drug-induced coma until more permanent arrangements could be made.

Of the many companies he gained control over that day, Colin acquired Nole's experimental cryogenic technology, intended to be used for human space travel. As Nole Fetor, Colin spearheaded final development of cryopods, then put them to use housing all of his previous host bodies in a new Pāra research facility built on Malcolm's estate in Mount Vernon. This included Monty, with Nole trapped inside. Out of respect Colin did not kill him, though it may have been a better alternative than this.

Chapter 28

Pandora's Box

There was one final, crucial question Malcolm needed answered: *How did Colin assume control over him?*

Done with this miserable dystopia, Malcolm returned to the comfort of the twenty-first century, arriving at a time just minutes after he would be returned to his physical form. Any closer and he feared he would be thrust back into his body before he could ascertain what was to happen to him..

Apparating to his present day, Malcolm found himself hovering over his neighbor's house. One that wouldn't last another couple of centuries before being demolished to make way to a victim trophy room – unless he could find a way to change the course of history.

From there, Malcolm returned to his panic room in time to see Monty dragging his body out of the bedroom and down the hallway. Colin had ambushed him during or just after *this* surrection. He dragged his limp body through the front door and into the back of Monty's dark SUV.

There was no return.

Malcolm now knew now what he must do. Colin was proof that humankind wasn't ready for this god-like power.

Malcolm's lifelong pursuit, surrection, was a Pandora's box. Opening it fundamentally changed the global power structure, placing unprecedented power into the hands of an apathetic narcissist beholden to the addiction of affirmation and flattery, leading to a world with more sorrow, vice, violence, greed, madness and death. And that was just one man. Zeus also secretly added hope to Pandora's box to help people survive. In this case, that hope was that surrection would be used to advance human understanding of the universe we live in, the physical mechanisms and spiritual aspects that life is made of, in to better humanity.

Surrection also granted Malcolm the ability to go back in time to close Pandora's box before it ever opened. Solemnly, this was the choice that Malcolm made – to sacrifice one of humanity's greatest discoveries in order to save the world from the chaos and misery it brought.

Malcolm planned his moment.

He traveled back to the beginning: The day he first trialed serum #134. As the audio progressed through its sequence, he lay in wait. At the exact moment he first surrected, his older self immediately jumped into his body, and just as

Colin had hijacked others, he stole himself from himself. Malcolm's body arched, he let out a moan as he exhaled, and his arms involuntarily extended backward. He had done it. Malcolm had entered the physical world two weeks into the past.

With little hesitation, he walked out of the room, then returned as quickly as he left, went into Macy's laboratory in the kitchen of the guest house and got to work. He accessed Macy's files and her available substance inventory, determining the changes he had to make to turn serum #134 lethal. Importantly, he had to do it undetected. Colin could not know he had changed the serum. First modifying the documentation of the development of serum #134, Malcolm then added a lethal combination of PCP and ketamine to each vial in the refrigerator. Knowing that Colin would not review the footage for another couple of days, Malcolm accessed the surveillance footage and dubbed over the footage from when he returned to the room to when he left again. This time, his tracks appeared to be covered.

Repeating his life was an odd feeling. He had lived this moment in this body already. He was rewriting his own life, except his actions were different this time. He wouldn't pull the all-nighter he had last time, but he would take a vial of serum #134 to his main residence and purposely do a poor job covering his tracks just like last time.

The next day Malcolm called Monty directly to cancel Project Surrection.   A businessman before his current role of CIA director, Monty understood Malcolm's decision that this venture just wasn't and wouldn't be profitable. His lifetime pet project, Malcolm had been told countless times to move on to something that was going to make him money. It was never a factor for him, but an excellent excuse to shut it all down now.

Monty directed Naomi to send a crew from the agency to load up Macy's laboratory equipment and government computers. Once they departed Malcolm's residence, it finally felt real. *If this doesn't work, there is no second chance,* he thought. *I can't hijack my body from myself again at the very same time.*

Minutes turned to hours. Hours turned to days. Malcolm continued to deal with the mental trauma of the worst part of humanity displayed by Colin corrupting his discovery of surrection. In order to prevent the world domination and hundreds of souls thrown into an eternal purgatory, he had folded time on top of itself. Life experienced over the last week no longer happened for anyone except him, and that took a heavy toll on Malcolm.

A week had passed, and Malcolm was beginning to grow accustomed to a life without purpose. He was always panned as a hedonist nepobaby with no goals by his family and for once he wanted to see what that would actually be like. He wouldn't be able to ignore his academic experience of substance use, but this time he was doing it recreationally, as a crutch to dealing with the trauma of the next week that never happened. One afternoon, Malcolm began to finally think that the disturbing future for the world that he witnessed, caused by his discovery, and had been prevented. The scores of souls violently detached from their bodies and placed in an eternal purgatory had been prevented.

Then Malcolm's phone rang.

"Hello," said Malcolm into the unknown as the caller ID said "private."
"Malcolm, its Monty. I have some terrible news, and I wanted to give it to you myself."
"Colin passed away last night. Alexandria PD are calling it an overdose."
"They will likely contact you. I wanted to give you time to prepare for that conversation and remind you that the nondisclosure agreement still in place," Monty continued.
"My condolences on the loss of your associate," he finished and disconnected the call.

Colin was found in Room 420 of the *Alexandrian* hotel, a needleless injector next to his body, and a lethal dose of PCP and ketamine in his system. Malcolm hoped that Colin surrected before his body died, a just retribution for the pain and suffering he would bring down upon countless others, without empathy or remorse, if given the chance. Of this Malcolm was certain. He had seen that future.

Given the ability to travel the stars, we would choose instead to stare downward and knowingly destroy the Earth for our own short-sighted gain. Humankind is not ready for surrection.

And perhaps we never will.

Malcolm took off the lid to the last vial of serum #134, ceremoniously poured the liquid into the flowers lining the front porch of his house, then tossed the vial into the trash, removing the last vestige of Project Surrection from the property.